Judge Kim and the Kids Court

The Doggie Defendant

written by **Milo Stone, Shawn Martinbrough,** and **Joseph P. Illidge**

illustrated by **Christopher Jordan**

Ready-to-Read *GRAPHICS*

Simon Spotlight
New York London Toronto Sydney New Delhi

SIMON SPOTLIGHT
An imprint of Simon & Schuster Children's Publishing Division
1230 Avenue of the Americas, New York, New York 10020
This Simon Spotlight edition January 2023
Text copyright © 2023 by Shawn Martinbrough, Milo Stone, and Joseph P. Illidge
Illustrations copyright © 2023 by Christopher Jordan
For information about special discounts for bulk purchases, please contact
Simon & Schuster Special Sales at 1-866-506-1949 or business@simonandschuster.com.
Manufactured in the United States of America 1222 LAK
2 4 6 8 10 9 7 5 3 1
Cataloging-in-Publication Data for this title is available from the Library of Congress.
ISBN 978-1-6659-1967-8 (hc)
ISBN 978-1-6659-1966-1 (pbk)
ISBN 978-1-6659-1968-5 (ebook)

Cast of Characters

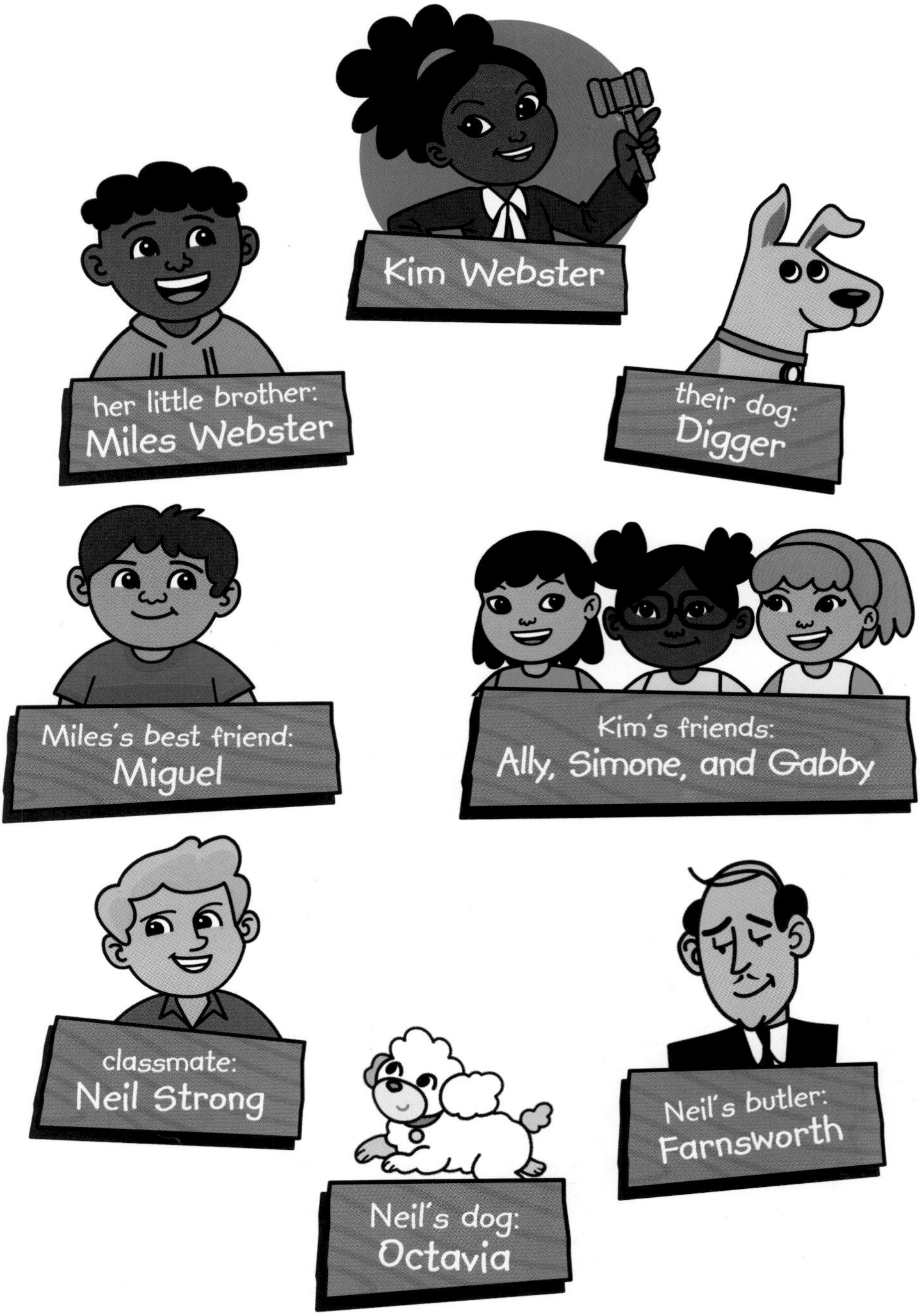
Kim Webster
her little brother:
Miles Webster
their dog:
Digger
Miles's best friend:
Miguel
Kim's friends:
Ally, Simone, and Gabby
classmate:
Neil Strong
Neil's butler:
Farnsworth
Neil's dog:
Octavia

This is Kim. She's here to give you some tips on reading this book.

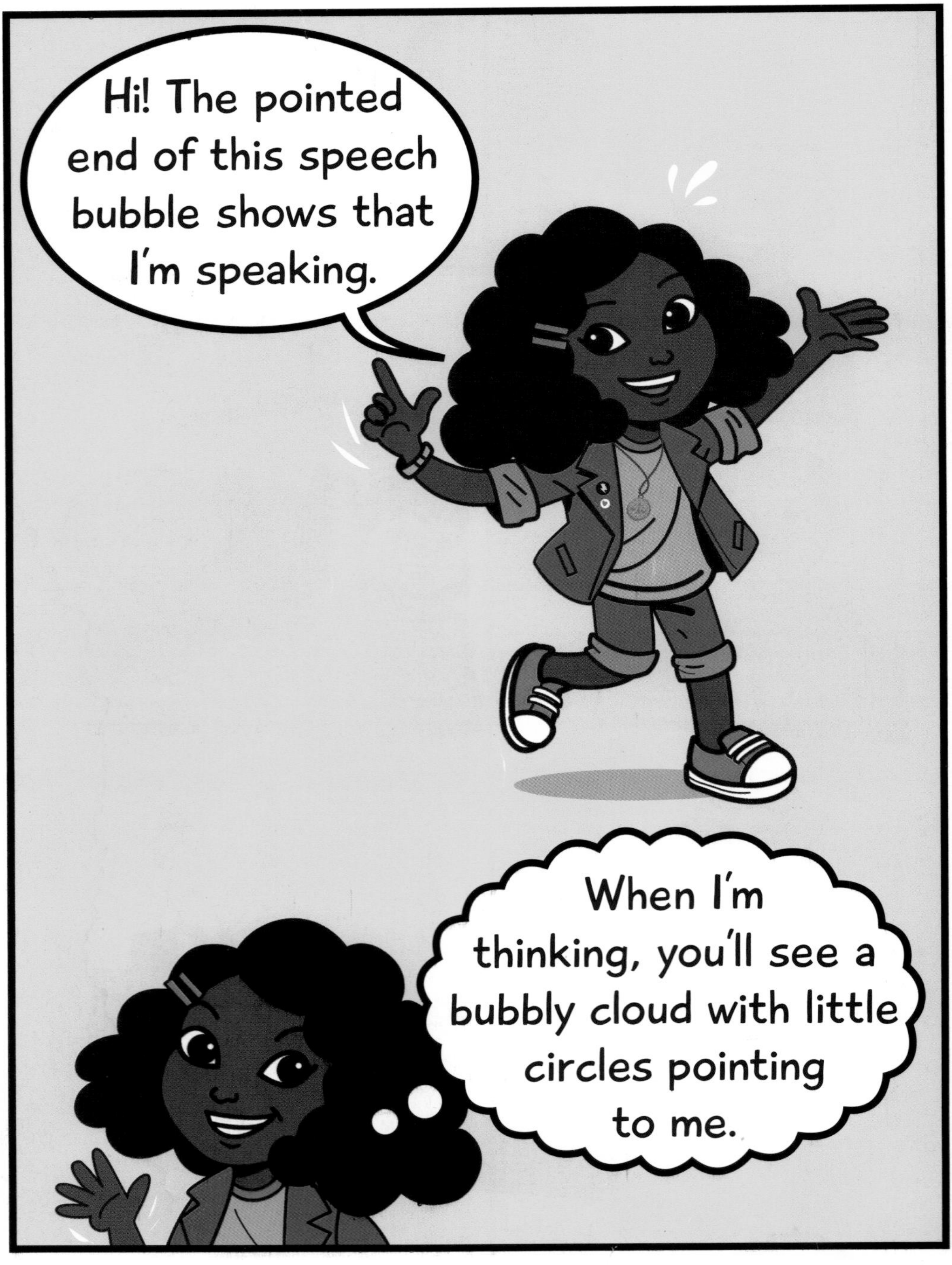
Hi! The pointed end of this speech bubble shows that I'm speaking.
When I'm thinking, you'll see a bubbly cloud with little circles pointing to me.

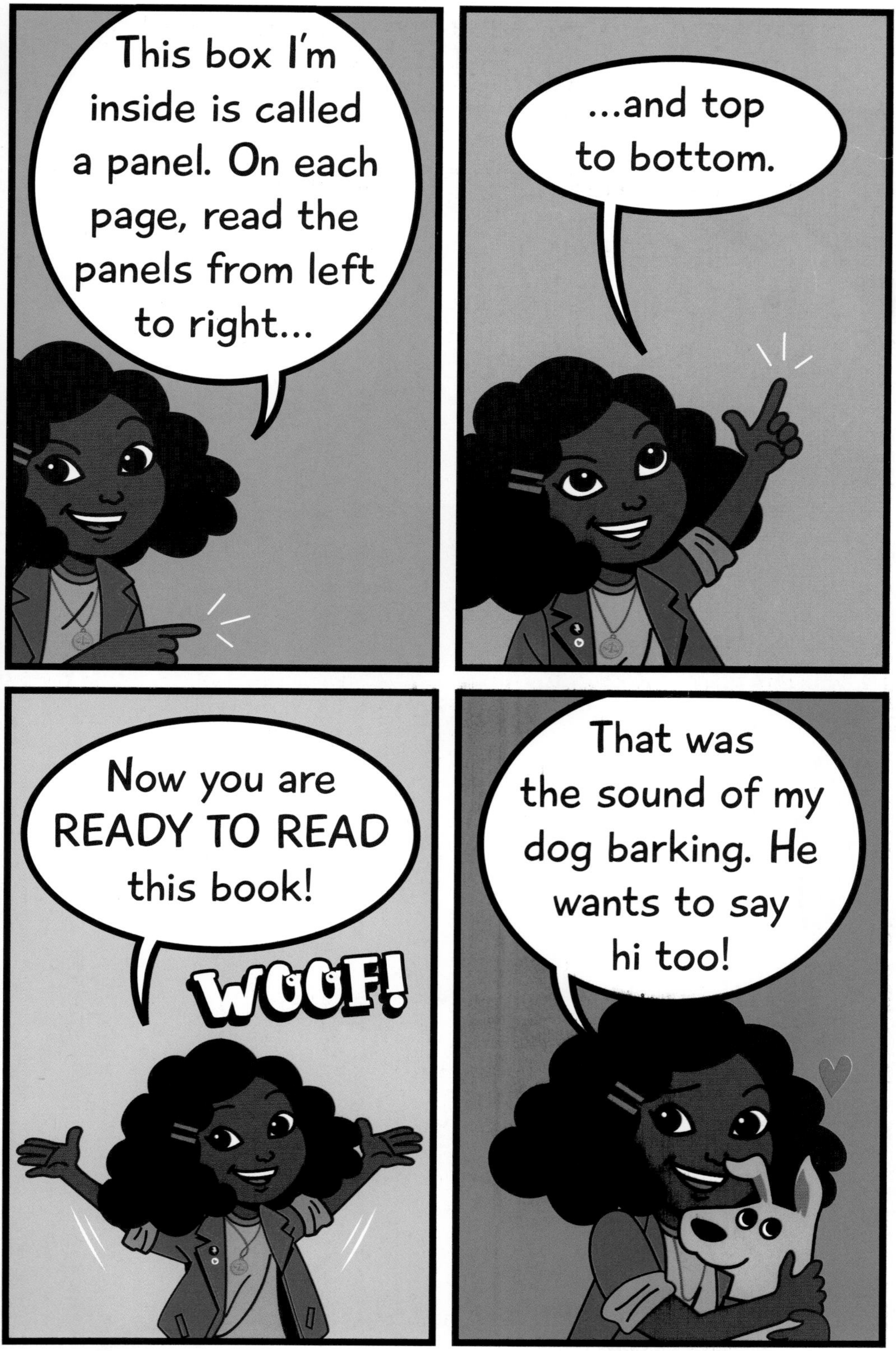
This box I'm inside is called a panel. On each page, read the panels from left to right...
...and top to bottom.
Now you are READY TO READ this book!
WOOF!
That was the sound of my dog barking. He wants to say hi too!

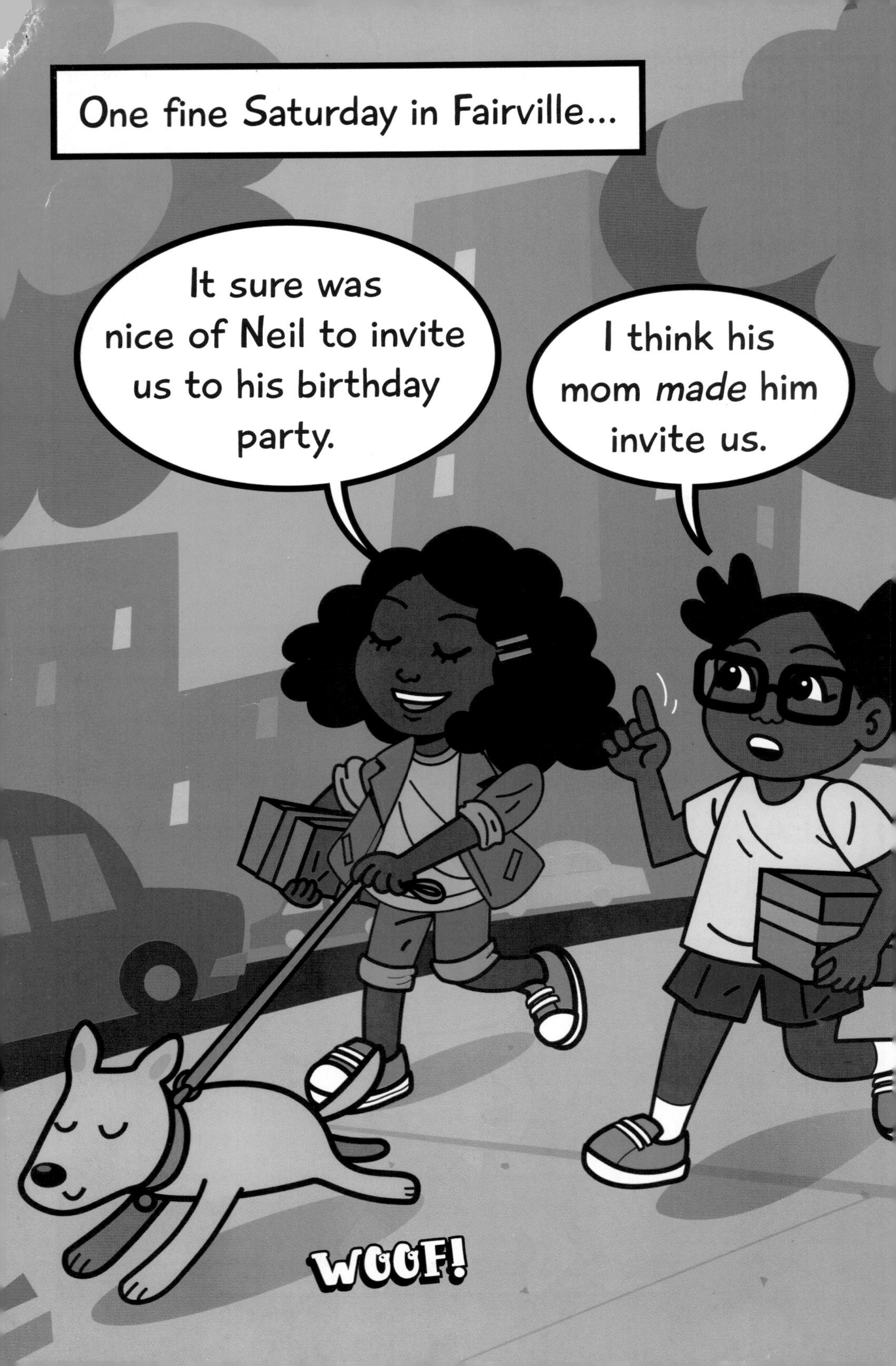
One fine Saturday in Fairville...
It sure was nice of Neil to invite us to his birthday party.
I think his mom *made* him invite us.
WOOF!

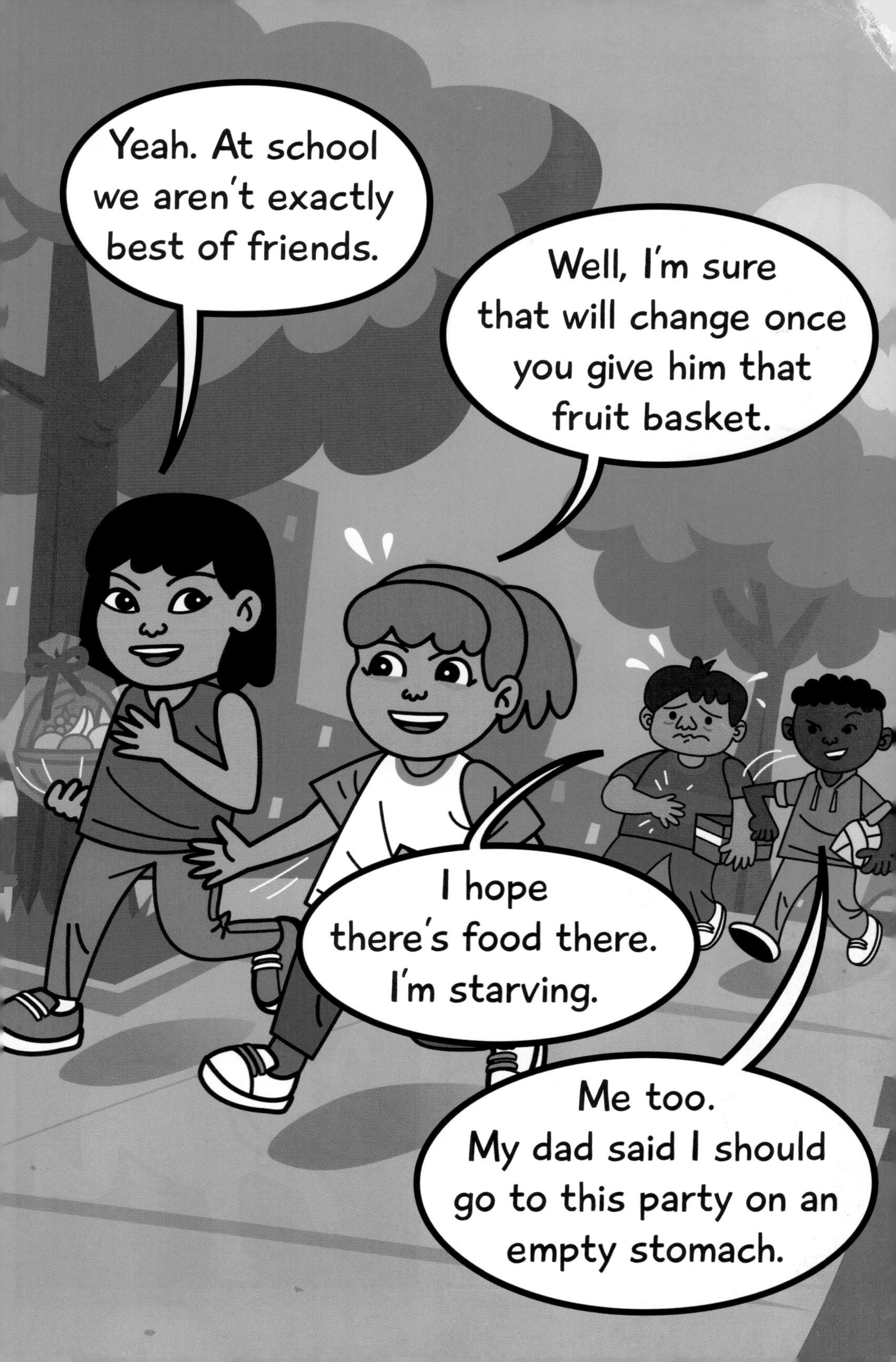
Yeah. At school we aren't exactly best of friends.
Well, I'm sure that will change once you give him that fruit basket.
I hope there's food there. I'm starving.
Me too. My dad said I should go to this party on an empty stomach.

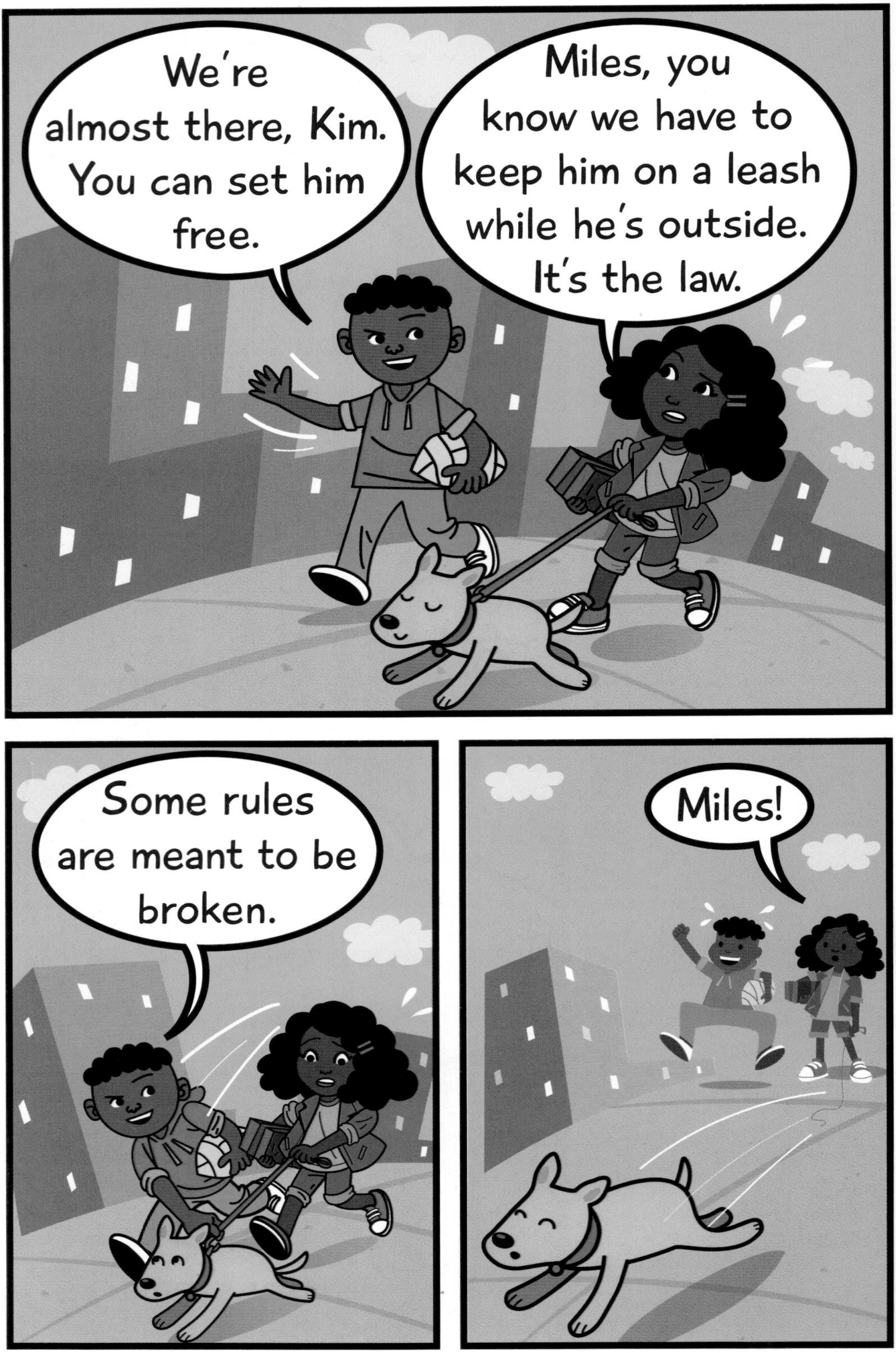
We're almost there, Kim. You can set him free.
Miles, you know we have to keep him on a leash while he's outside. It's the law.
Some rules are meant to be broken.
Miles!

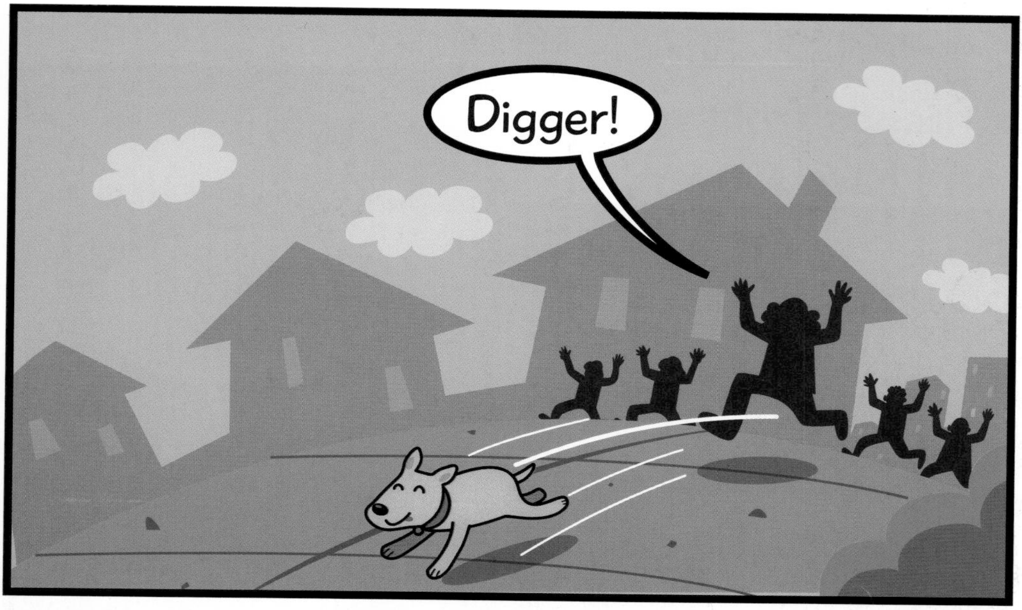
Digger!

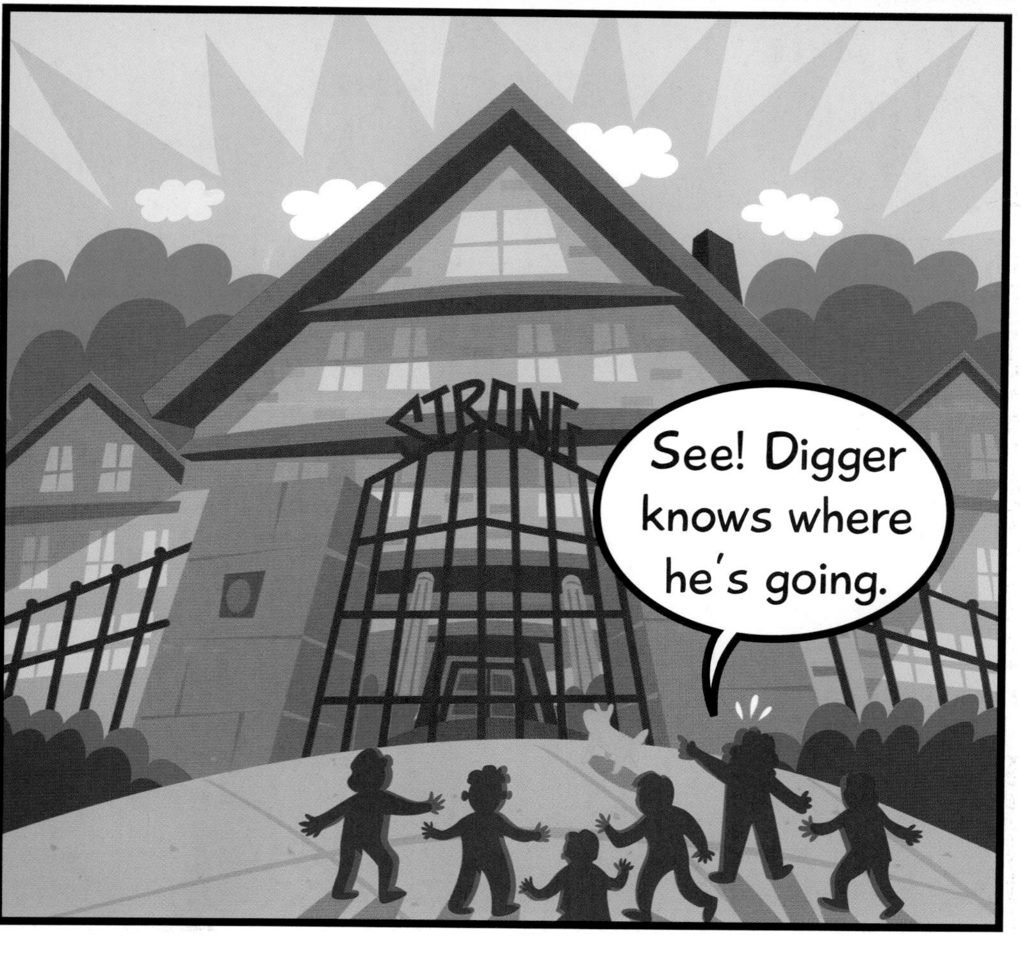
STRONG
See! Digger knows where he's going.

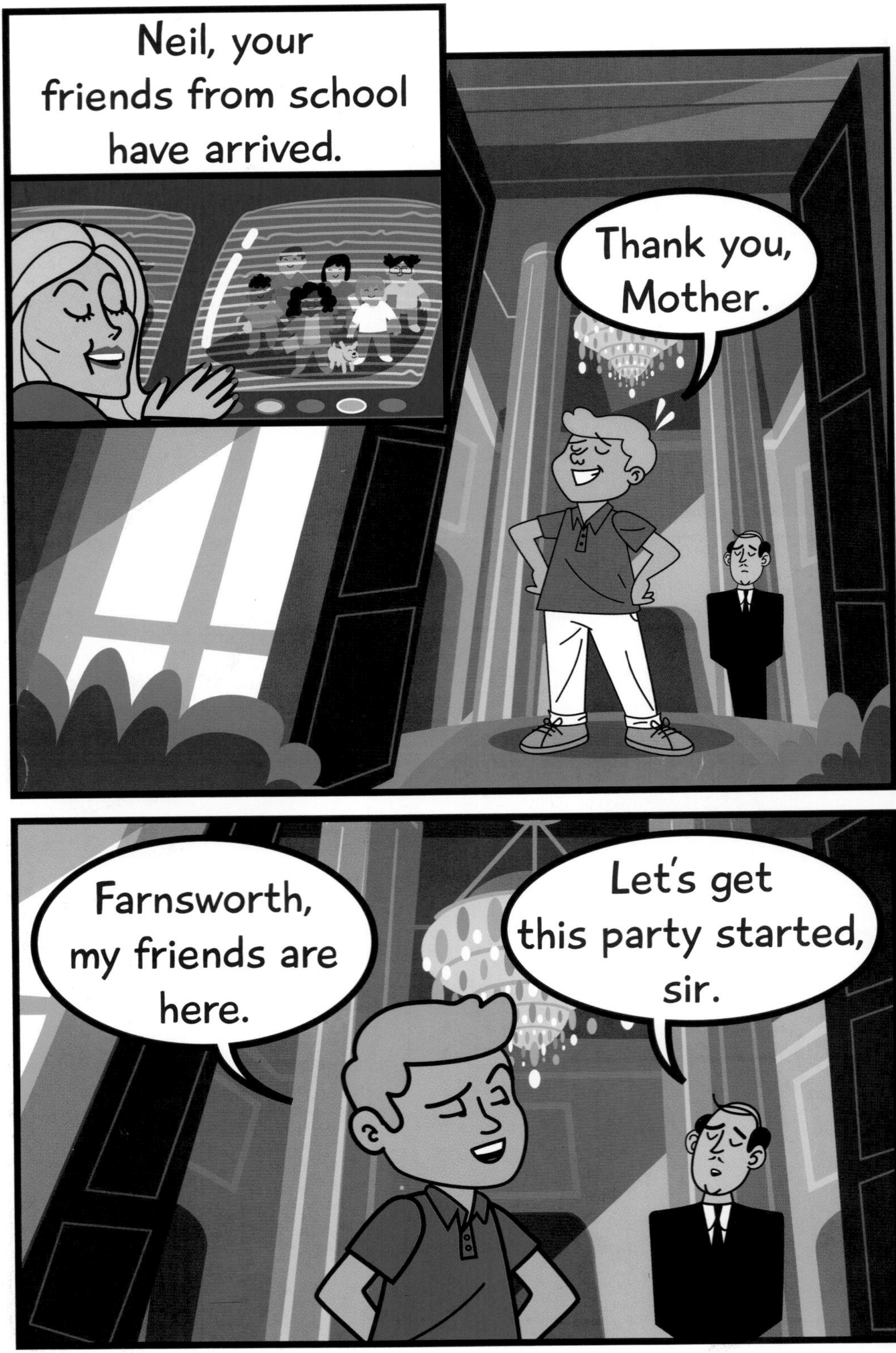
Neil, your friends from school have arrived.
Thank you, Mother.
Farnsworth, my friends are here.
Let's get this party started, sir.

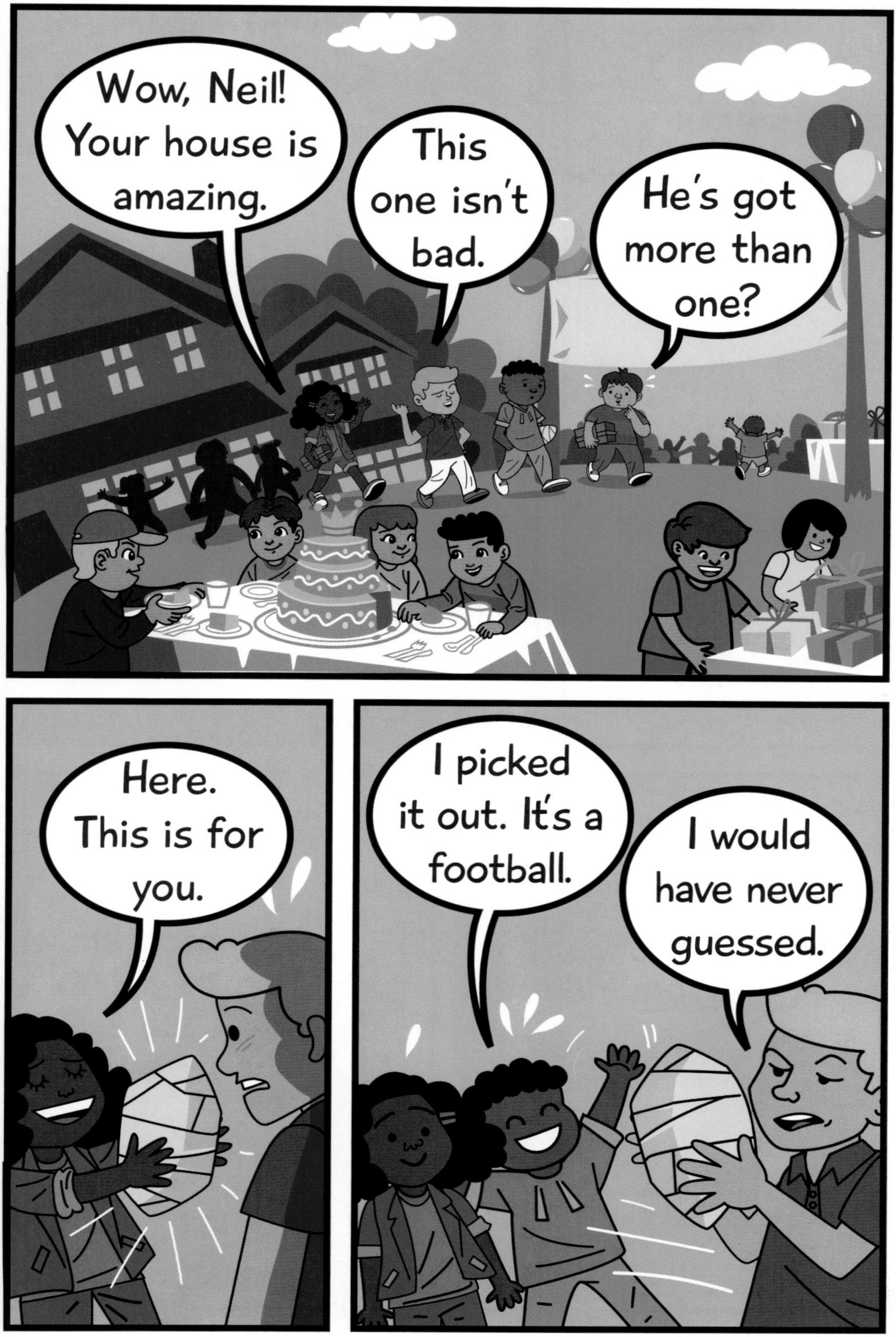
Wow, Neil! Your house is amazing.
This one isn't bad.
He's got more than one?
Here. This is for you.
I picked it out. It's a football.
I would have never guessed.

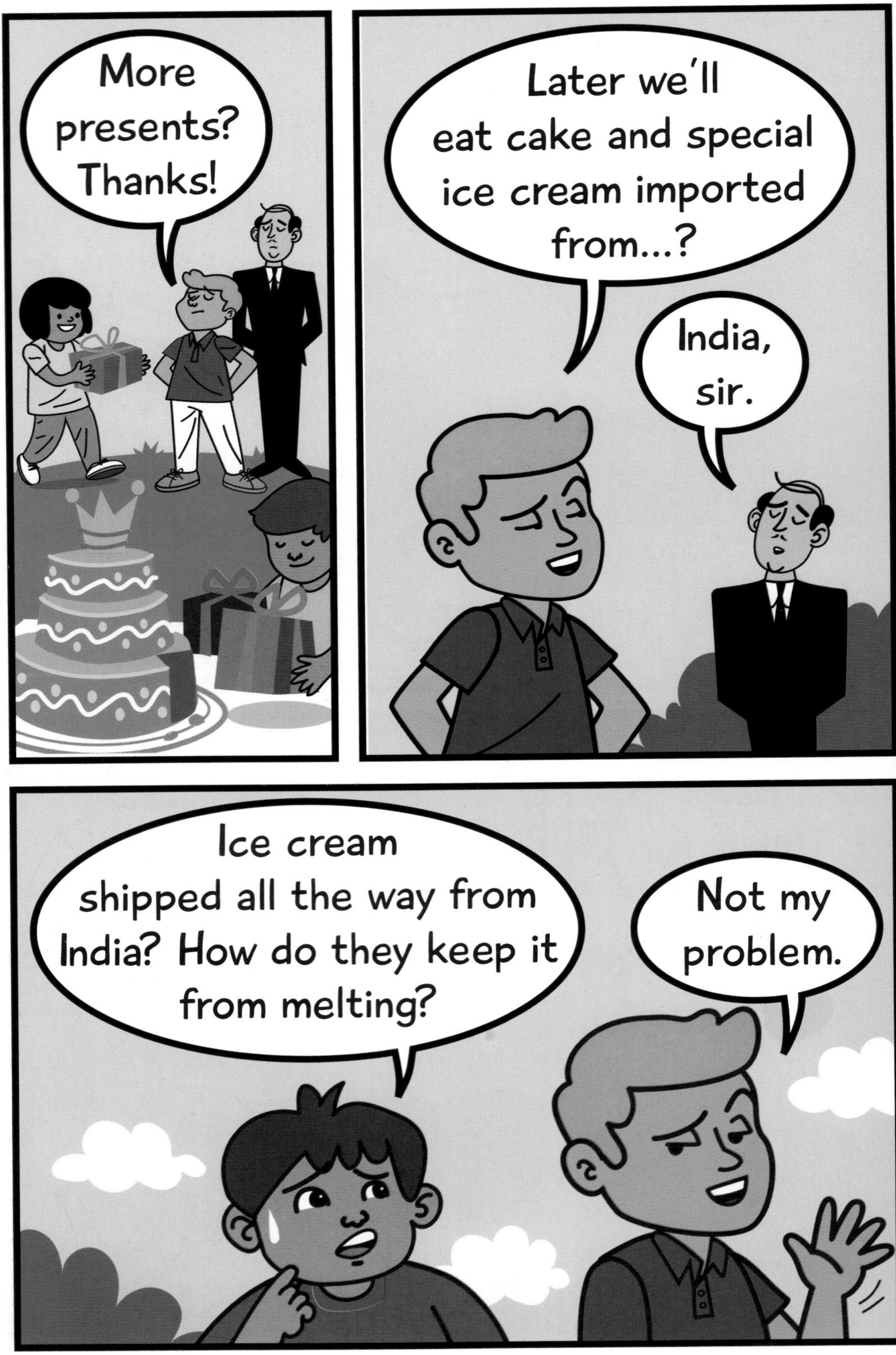
More presents? Thanks!
Later we'll eat cake and special ice cream imported from...?
India, sir.
Ice cream shipped all the way from India? How do they keep it from melting?
Not my problem.

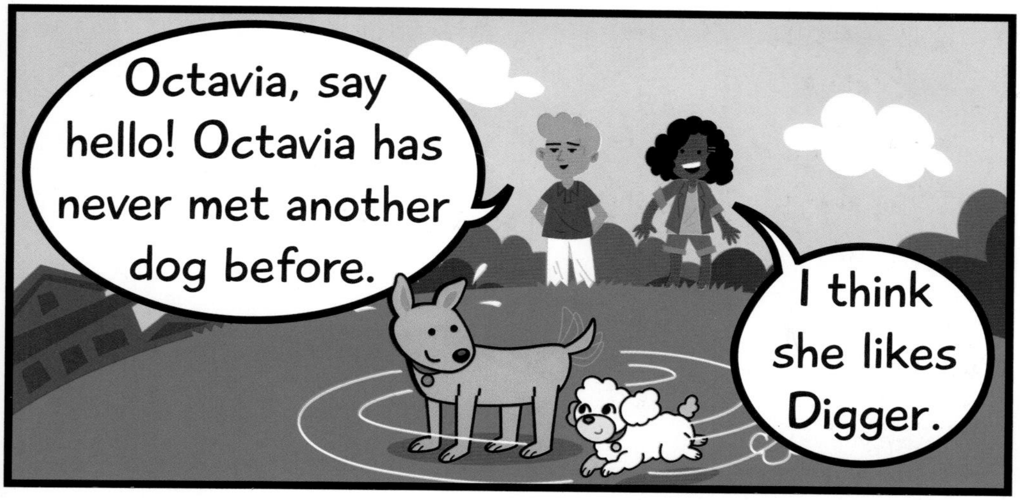
Octavia, say hello! Octavia has never met another dog before.
I think she likes Digger.

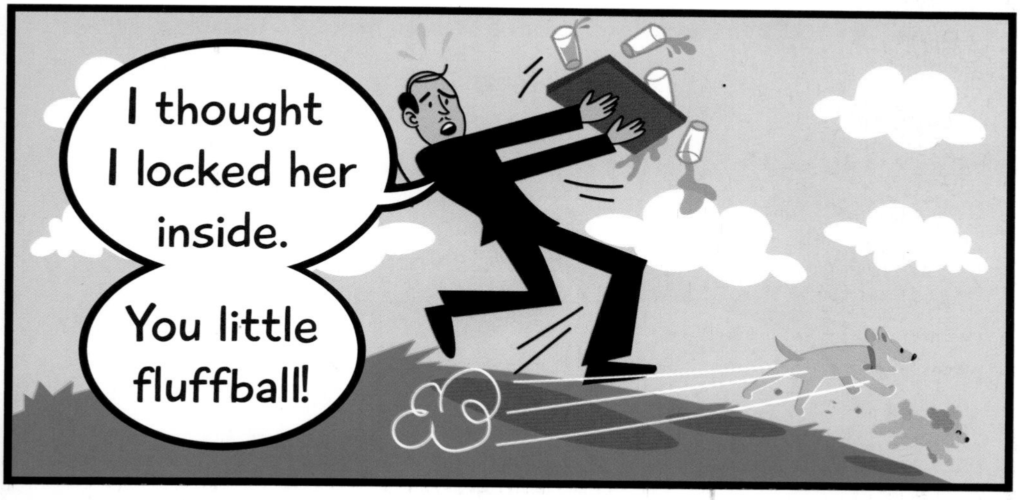
I thought I locked her inside.
You little fluffball!

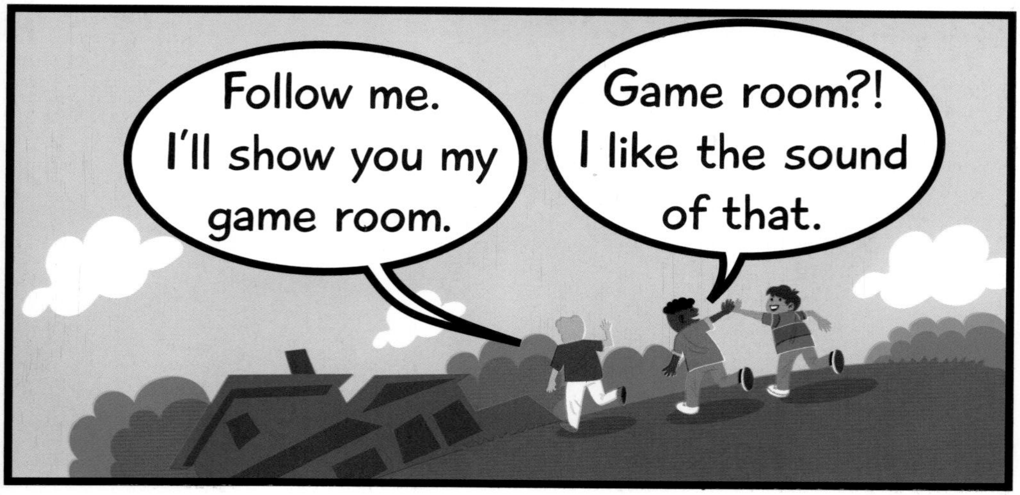
Follow me. I'll show you my game room.
Game room?! I like the sound of that.

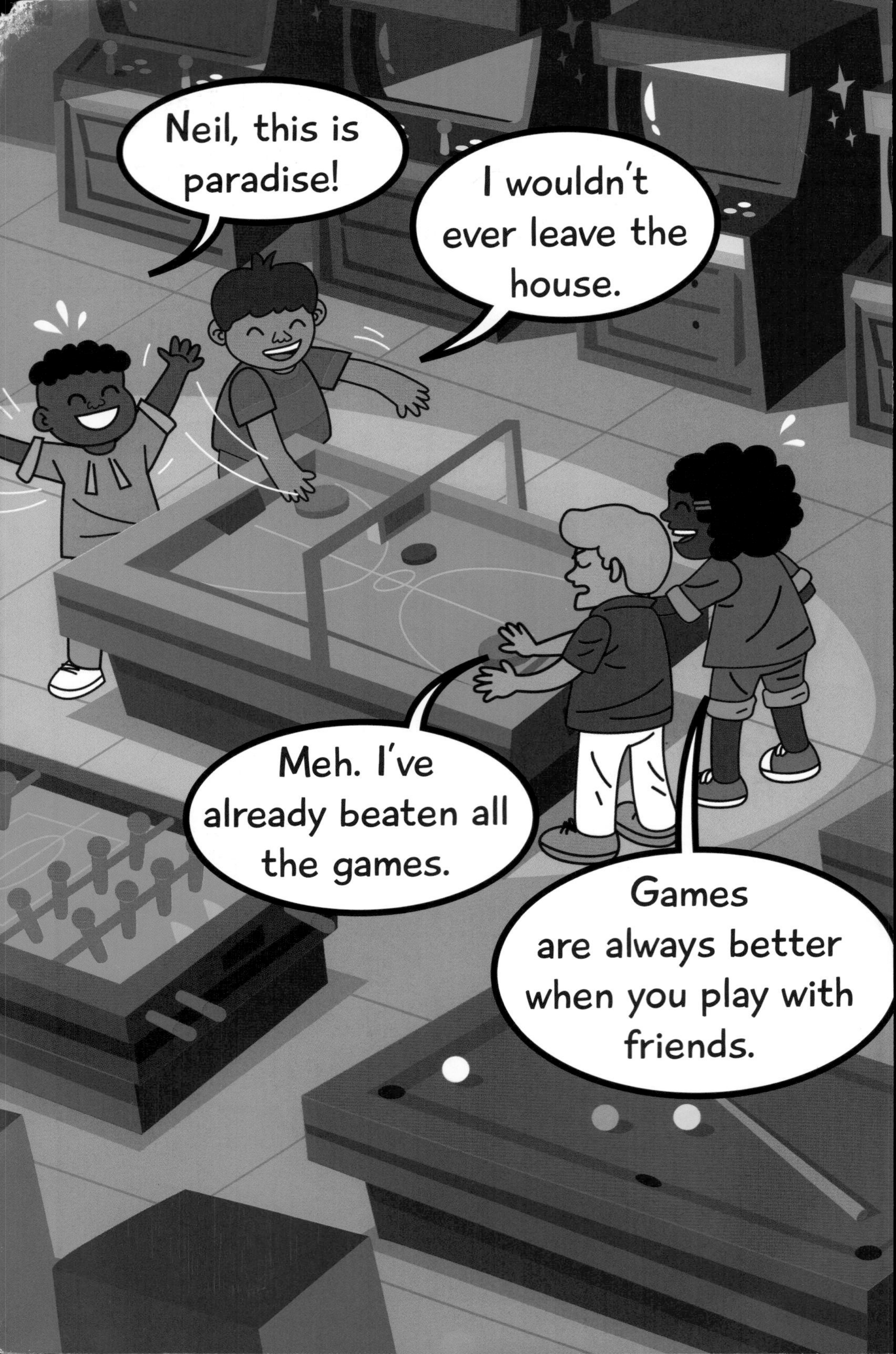
Neil, this is paradise!
I wouldn't ever leave the house.
Meh. I've already beaten all the games.
Games are always better when you play with friends.

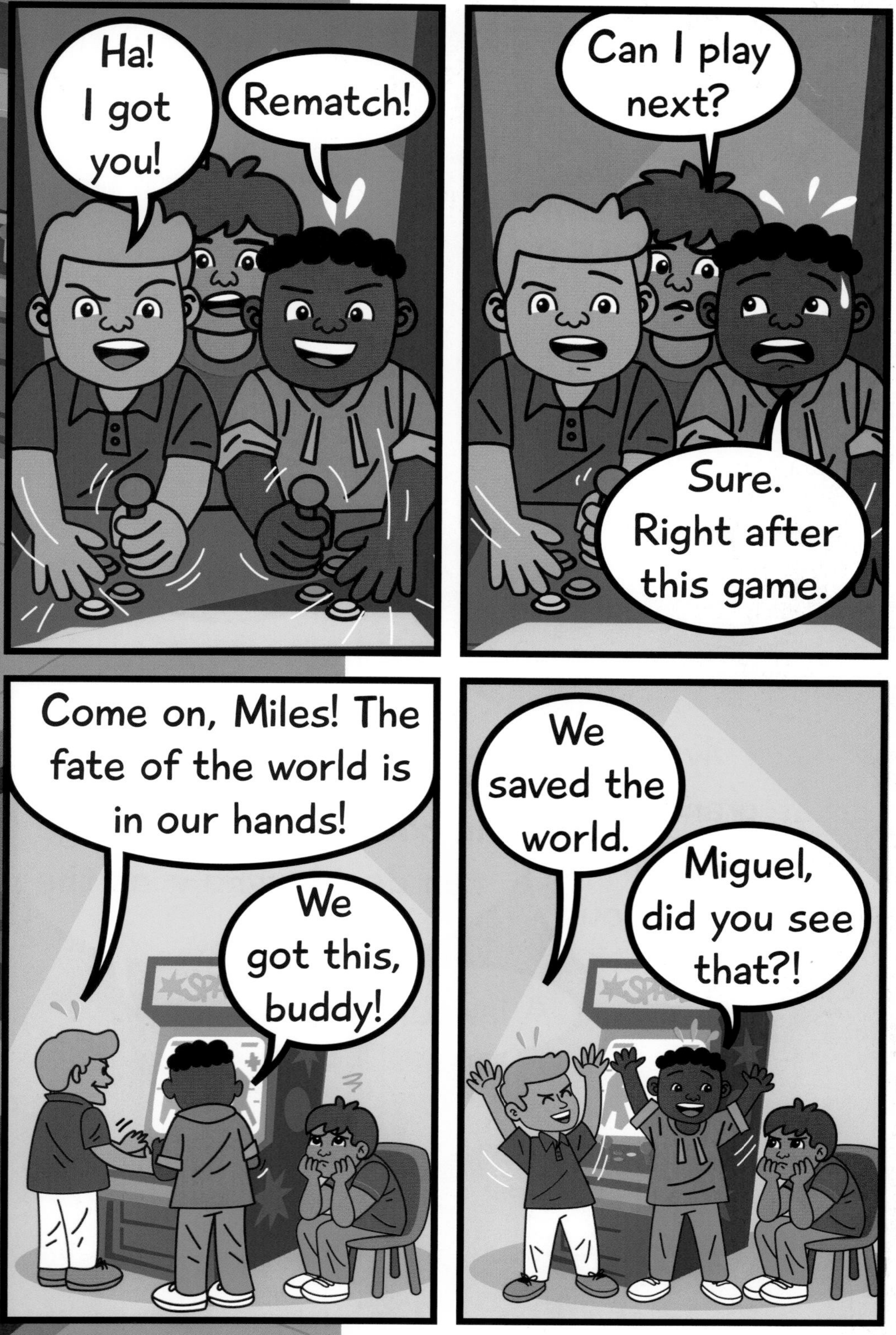
Ha! I got you!
Rematch!
Can I play next?
Sure. Right after this game.
Come on, Miles! The fate of the world is in our hands!
We got this, buddy!
We saved the world.
Miguel, did you see that?!

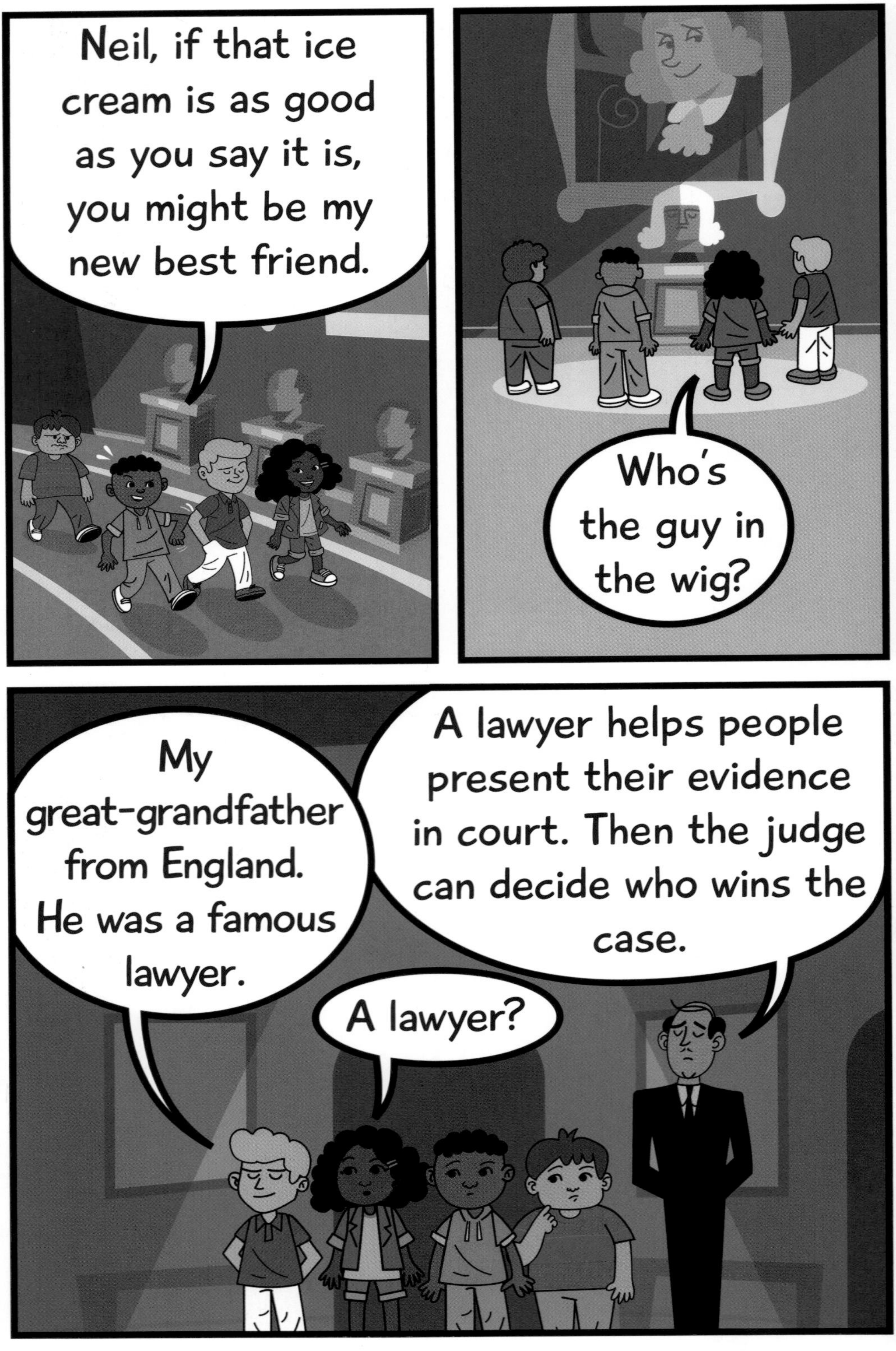
Neil, if that ice cream is as good as you say it is, you might be my new best friend.
Who's the guy in the wig?
My great-grandfather from England. He was a famous lawyer.
A lawyer?
A lawyer helps people present their evidence in court. Then the judge can decide who wins the case.

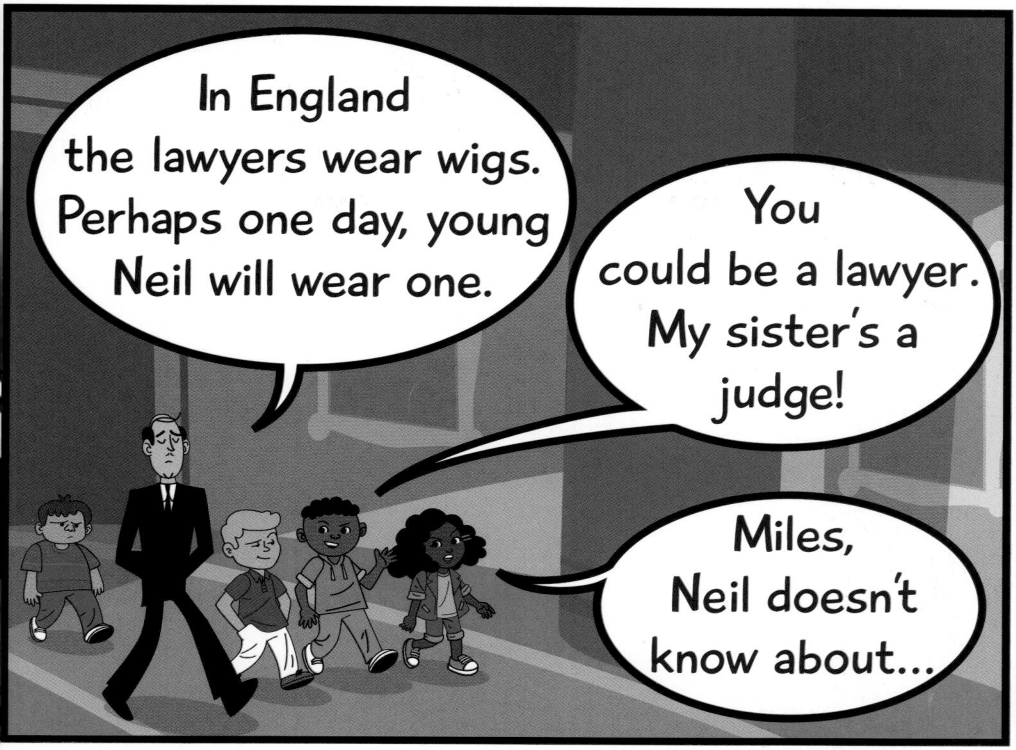
In England the lawyers wear wigs. Perhaps one day, young Neil will wear one.
You could be a lawyer. My sister's a judge!
Miles, Neil doesn't know about...

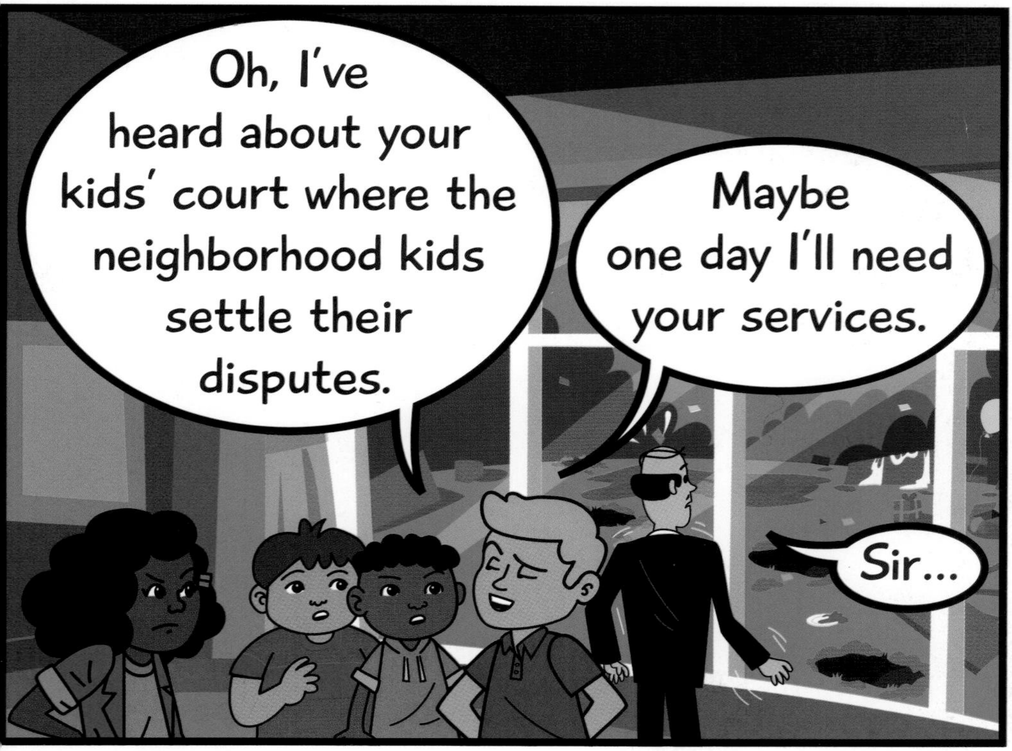
Oh, I've heard about your kids' court where the neighborhood kids settle their disputes.
Maybe one day I'll need your services.
Sir...

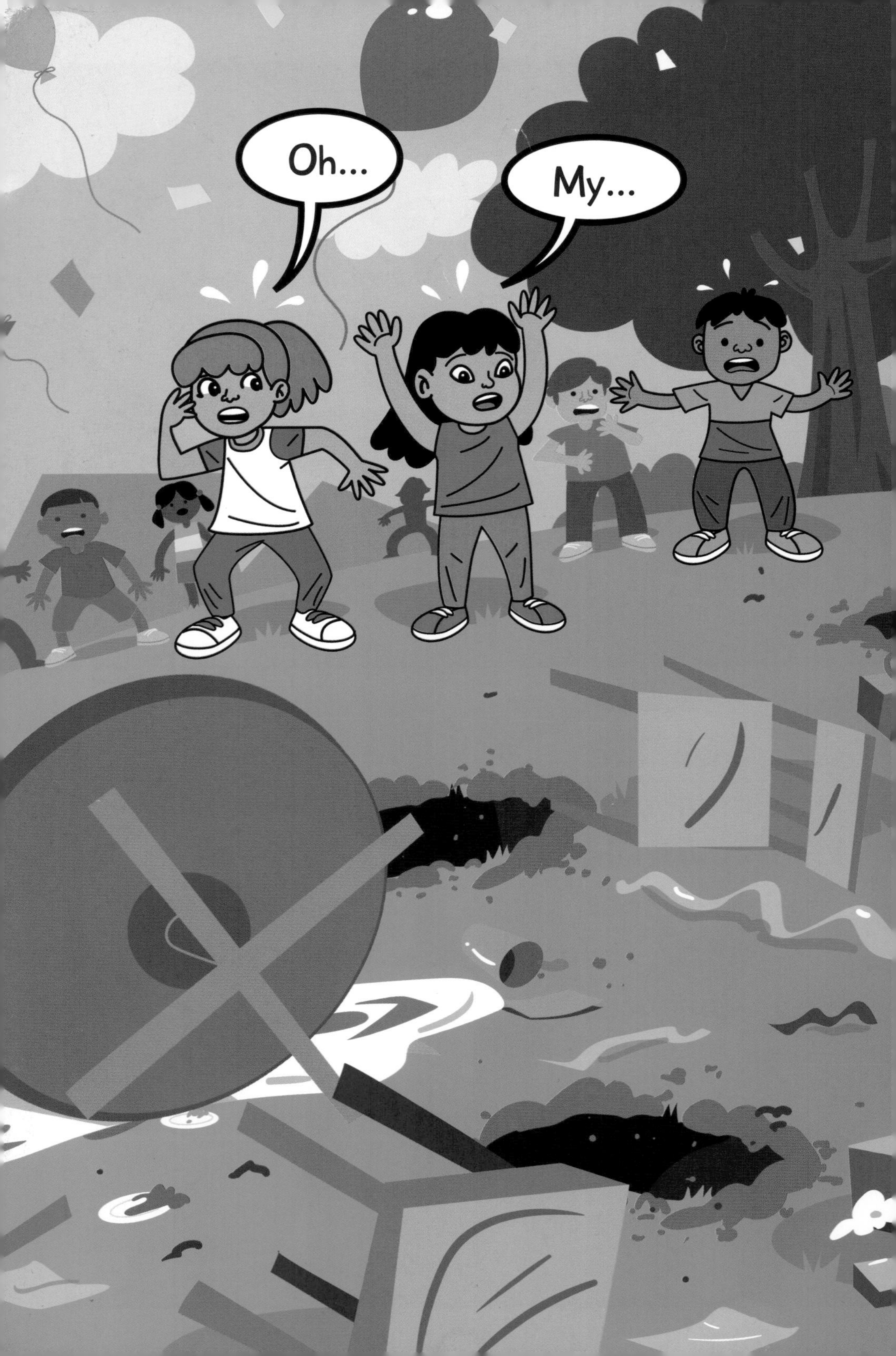
Oh...
My...

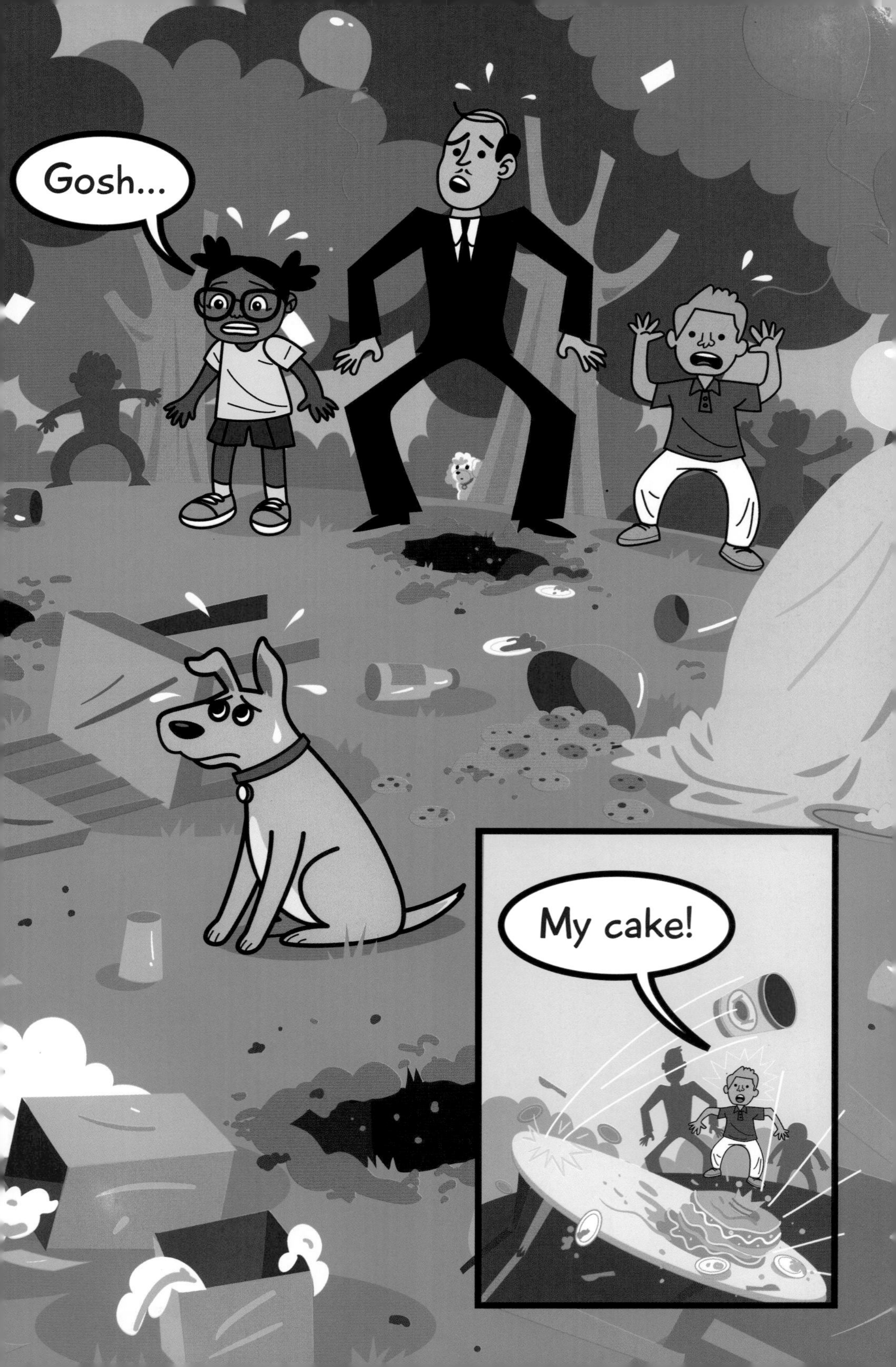
Gosh...
My cake!

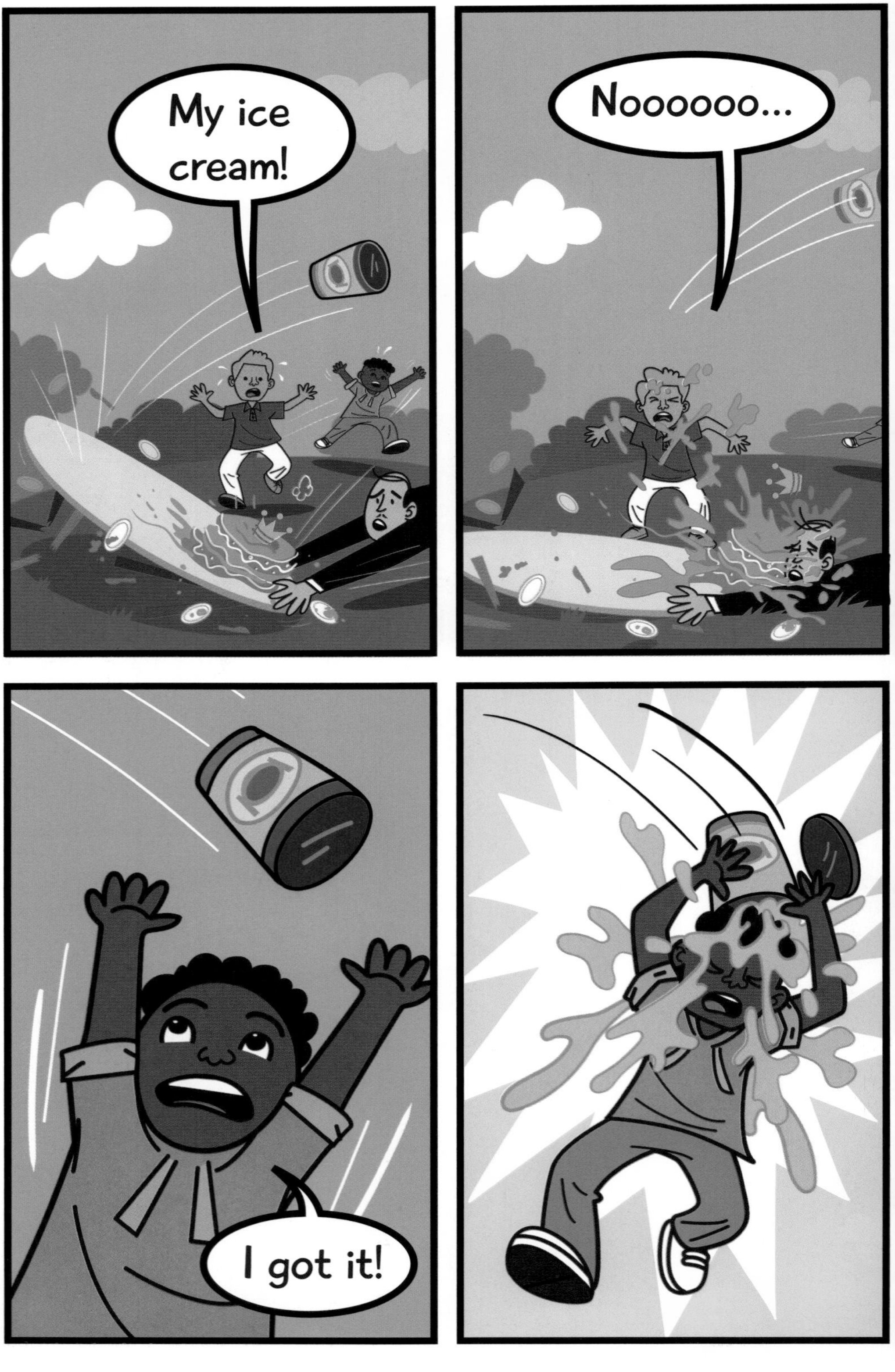
My ice cream!
Noooooo...
I got it!

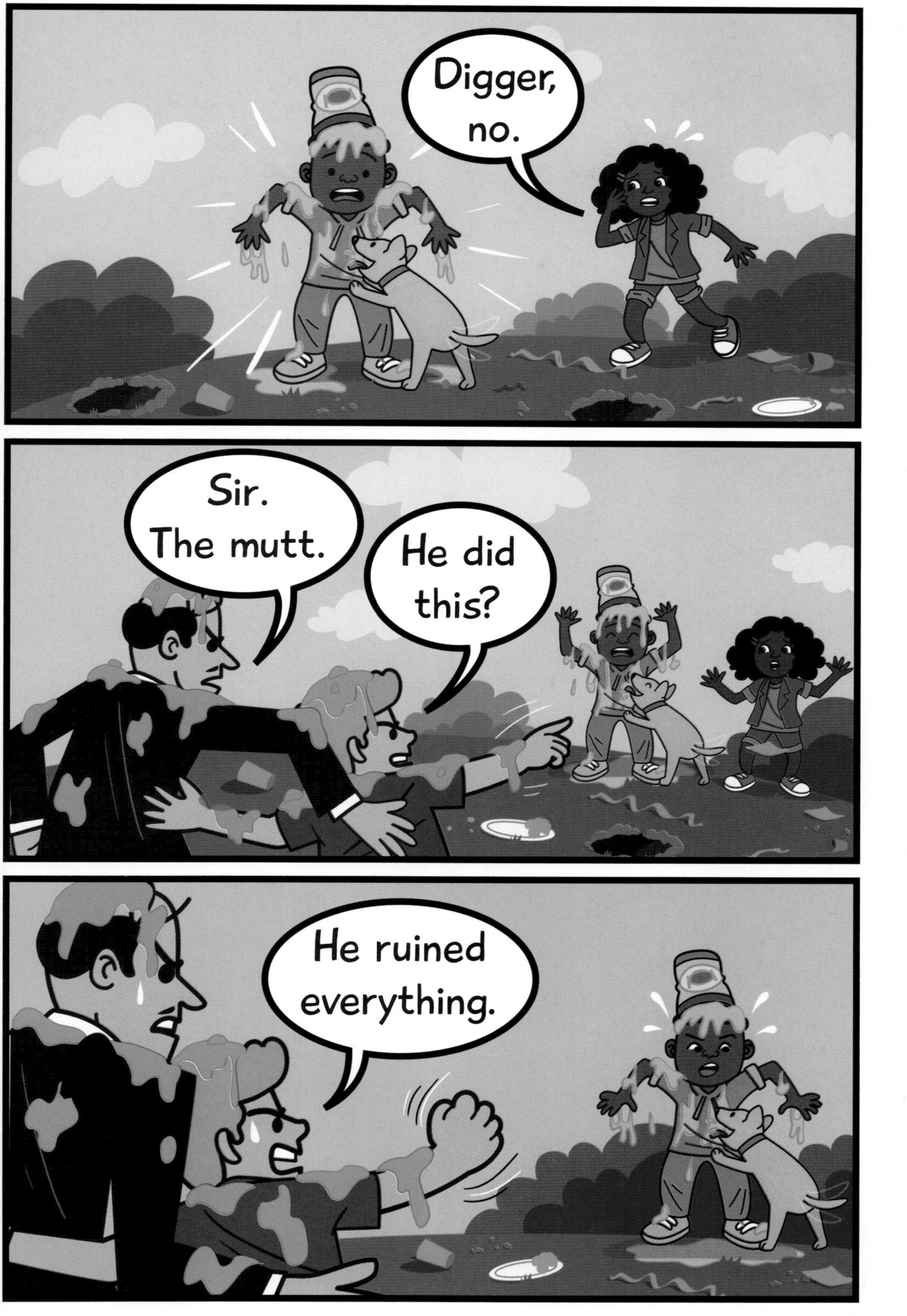
Digger, no.
Sir. The mutt.
He did this?
He ruined everything.

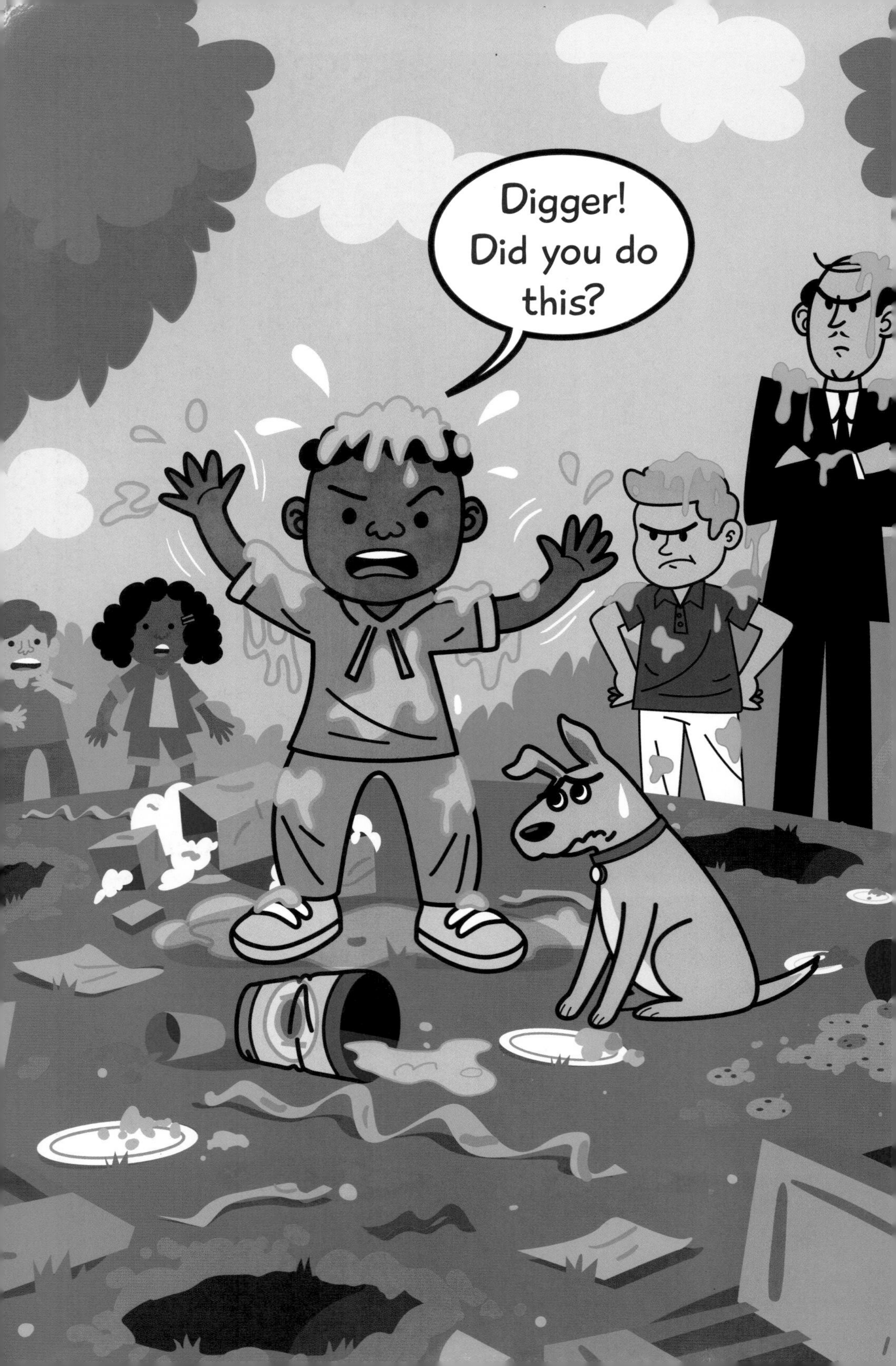
Digger! Did you do this?

Later at Kim's house...

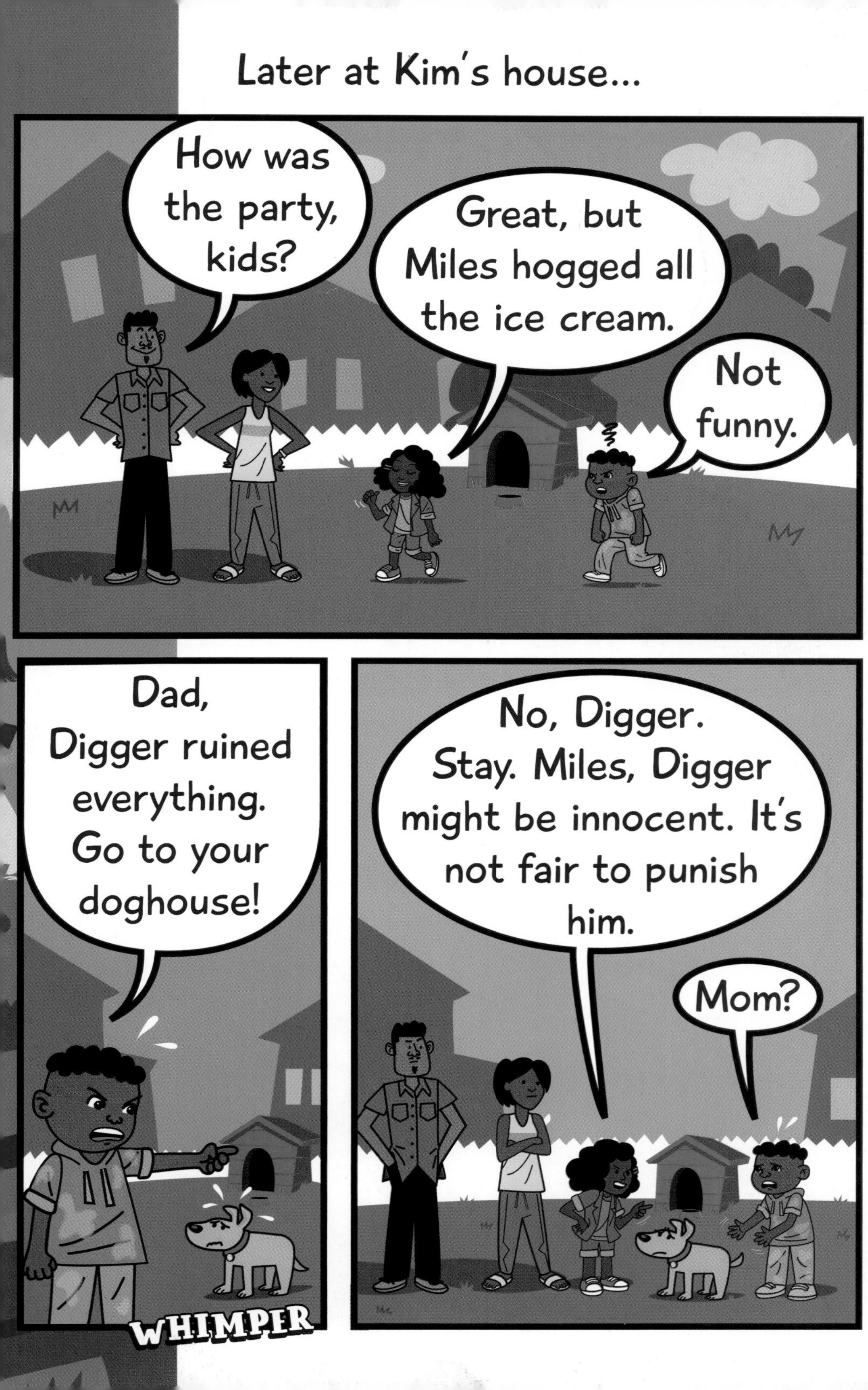
How was the party, kids?
Great, but Miles hogged all the ice cream.
Not funny.
Dad, Digger ruined everything. Go to your doghouse!
WHIMPER
No, Digger. Stay. Miles, Digger might be innocent. It's not fair to punish him.
Mom?

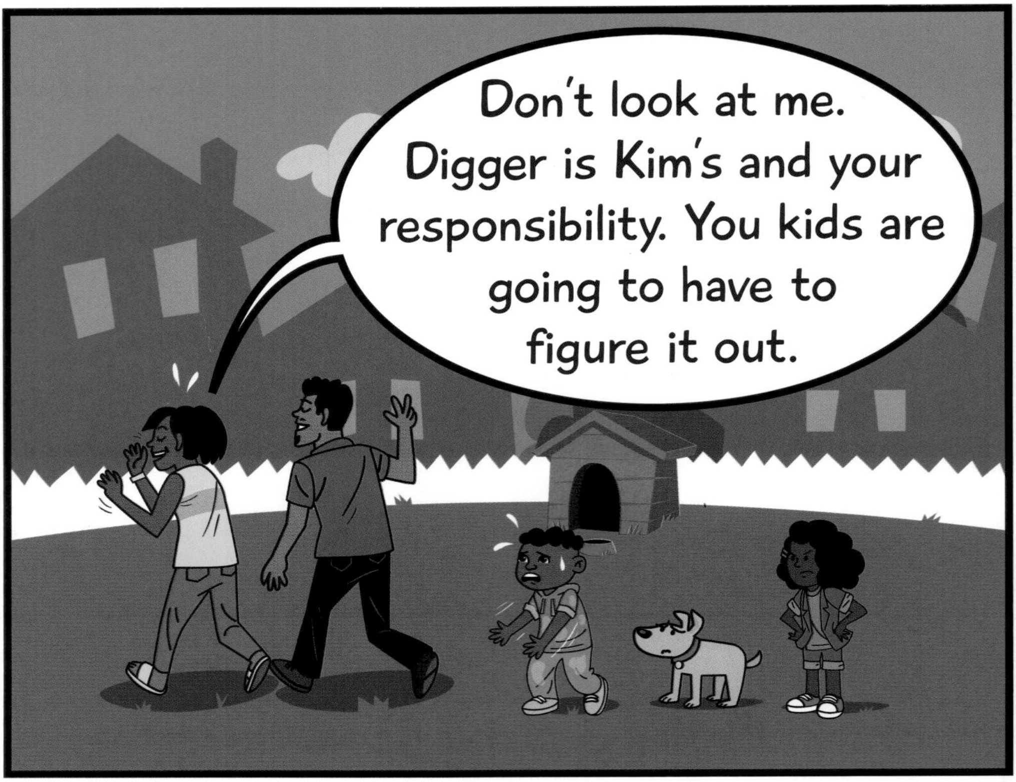
Don't look at me. Digger is Kim's and your responsibility. You kids are going to have to figure it out.

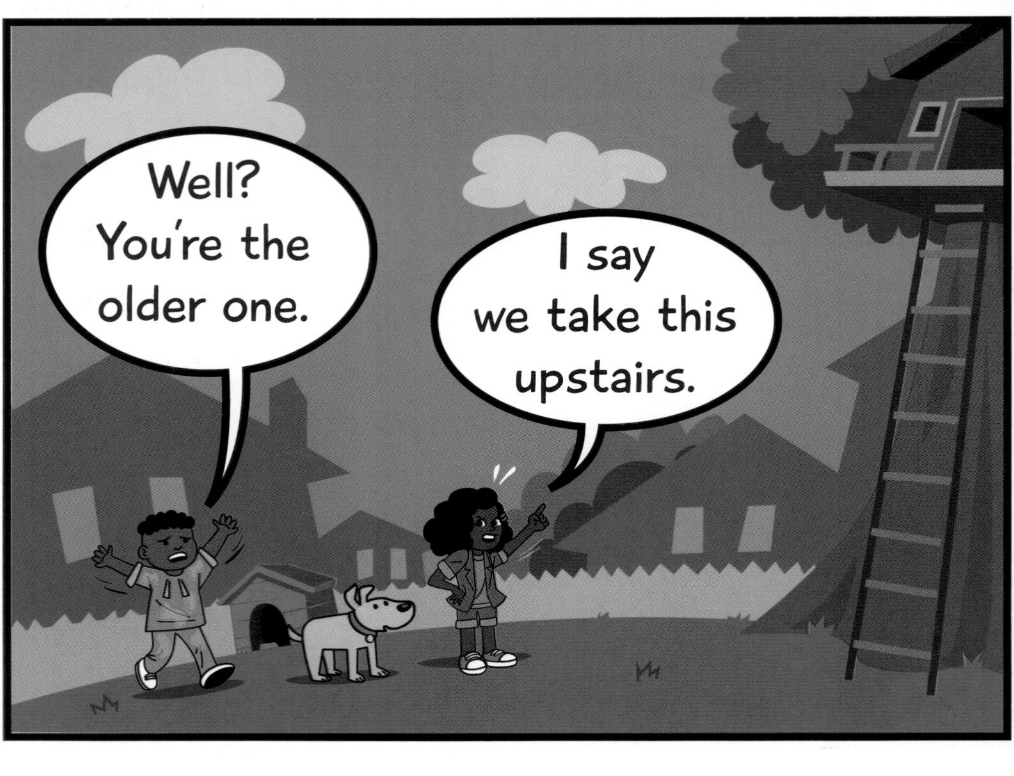
Well? You're the older one.
I say we take this upstairs.

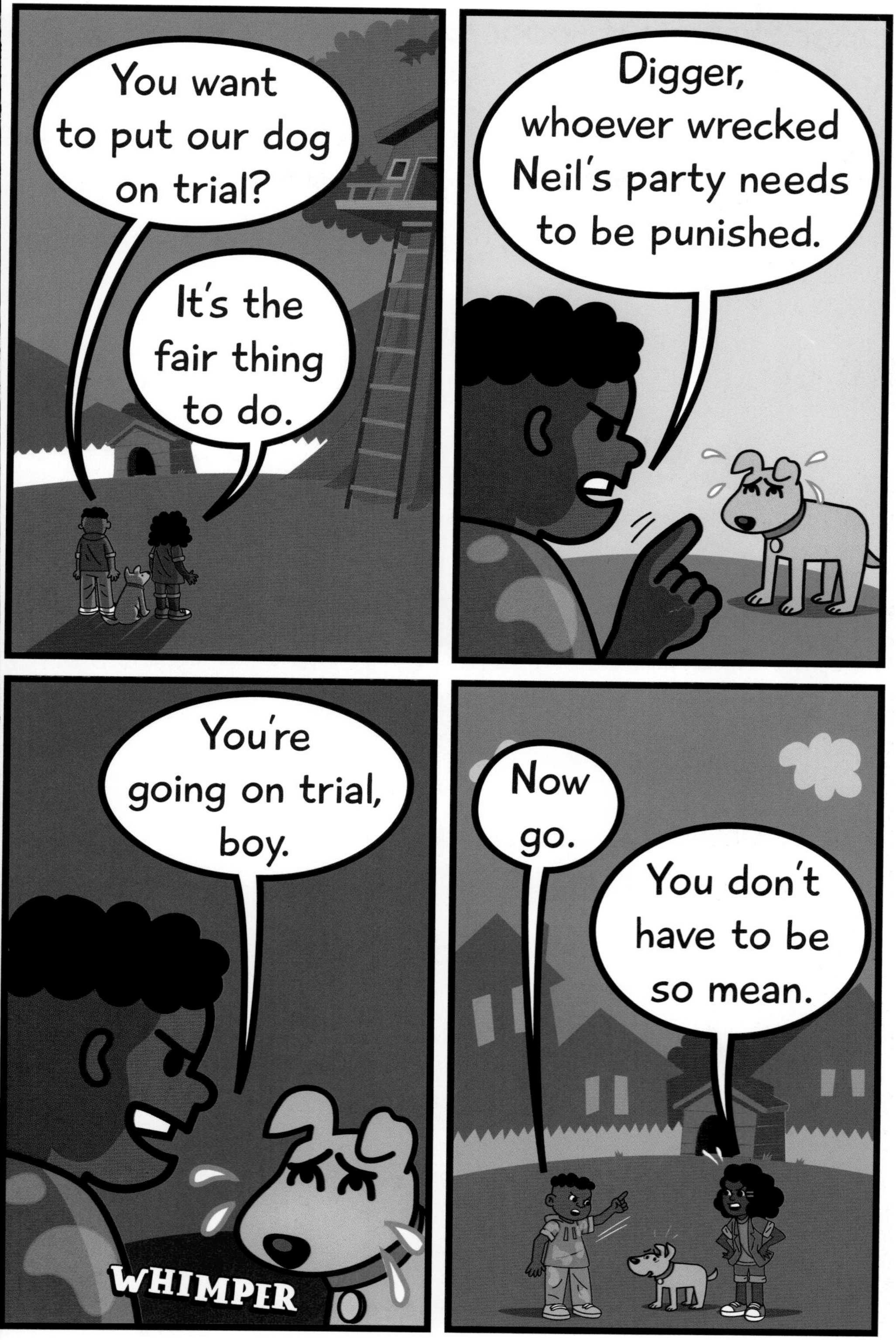
You want to put our dog on trial?
It's the fair thing to do.
Digger, whoever wrecked Neil's party needs to be punished.
You're going on trial, boy.
WHIMPER
Now go.
You don't have to be so mean.

Later that night, poor Digger has a nightmare...

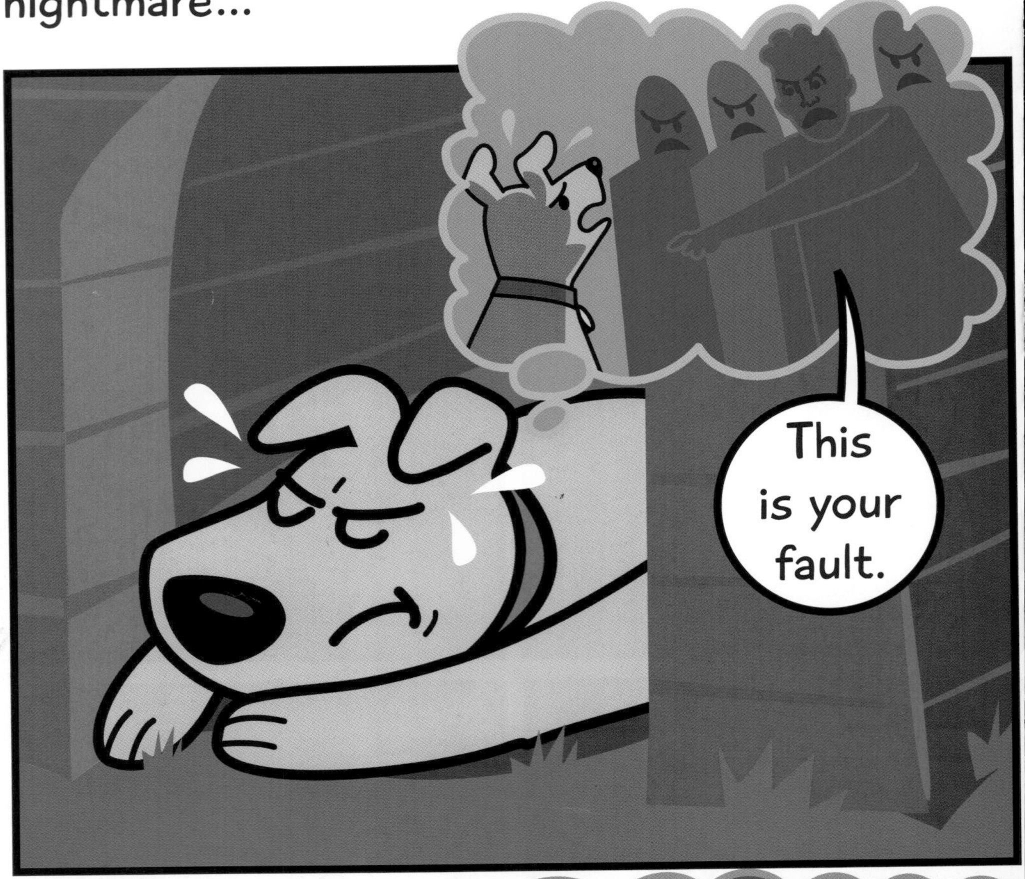
This is your fault.

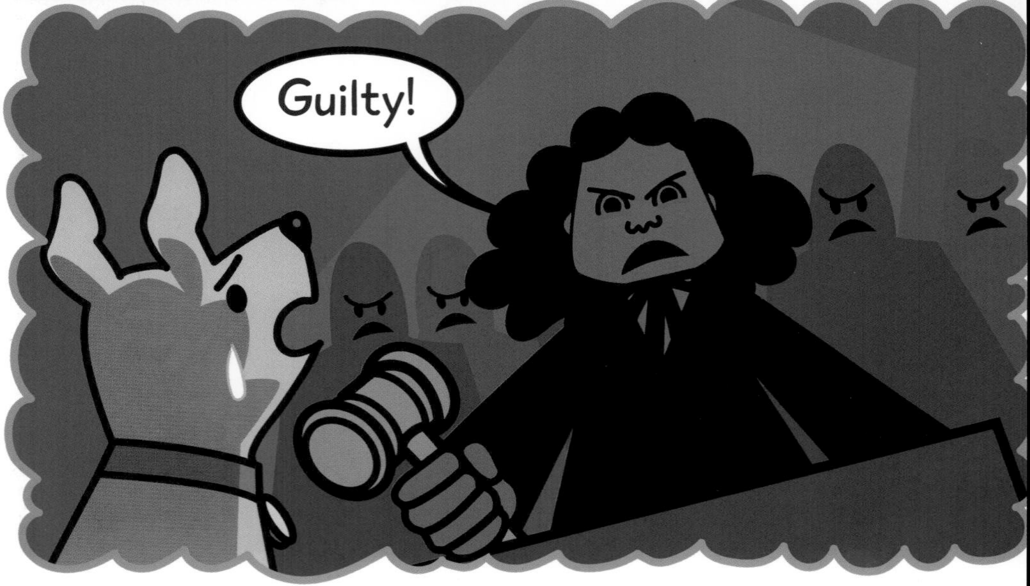
Guilty!

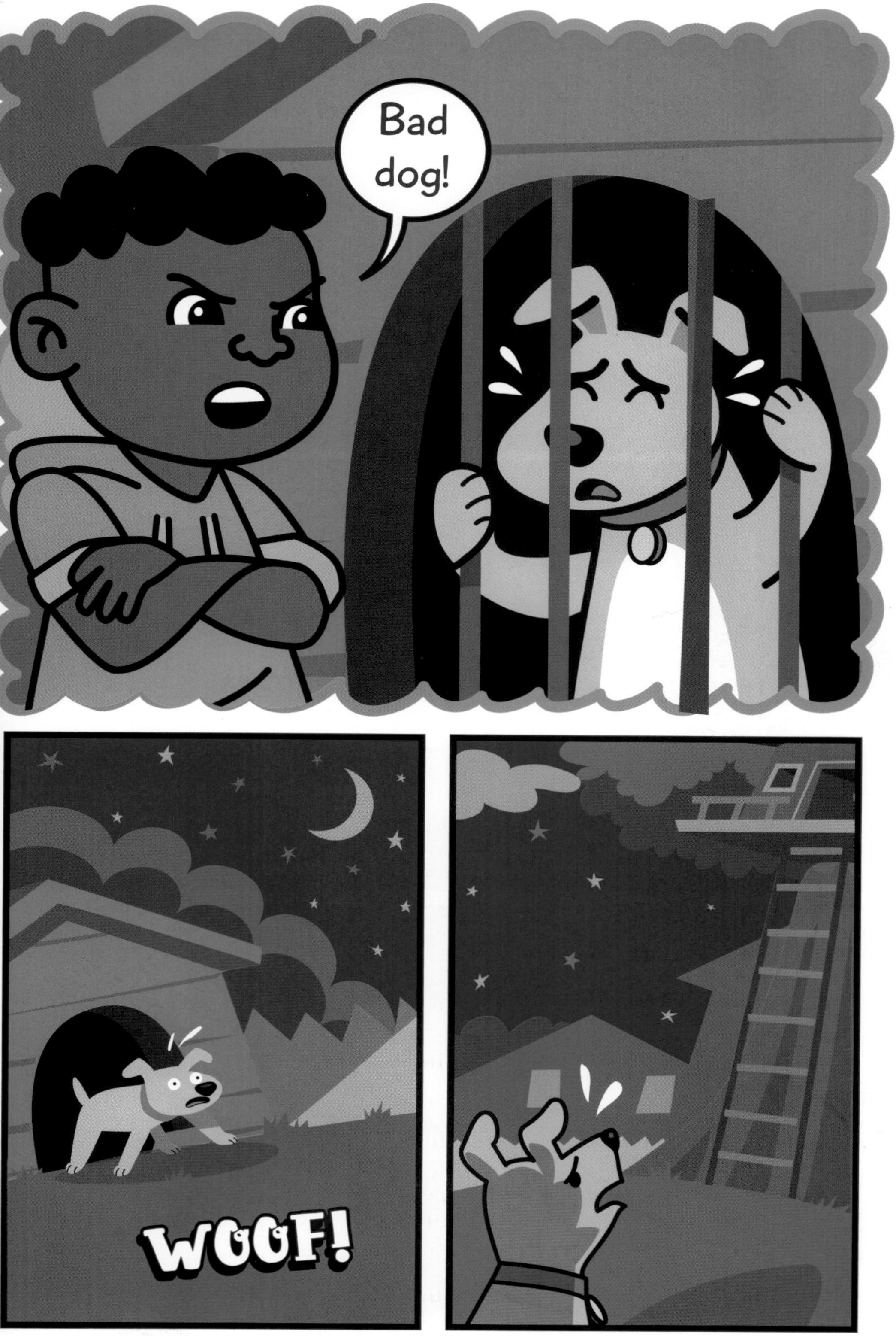
Bad dog!
WOOF!

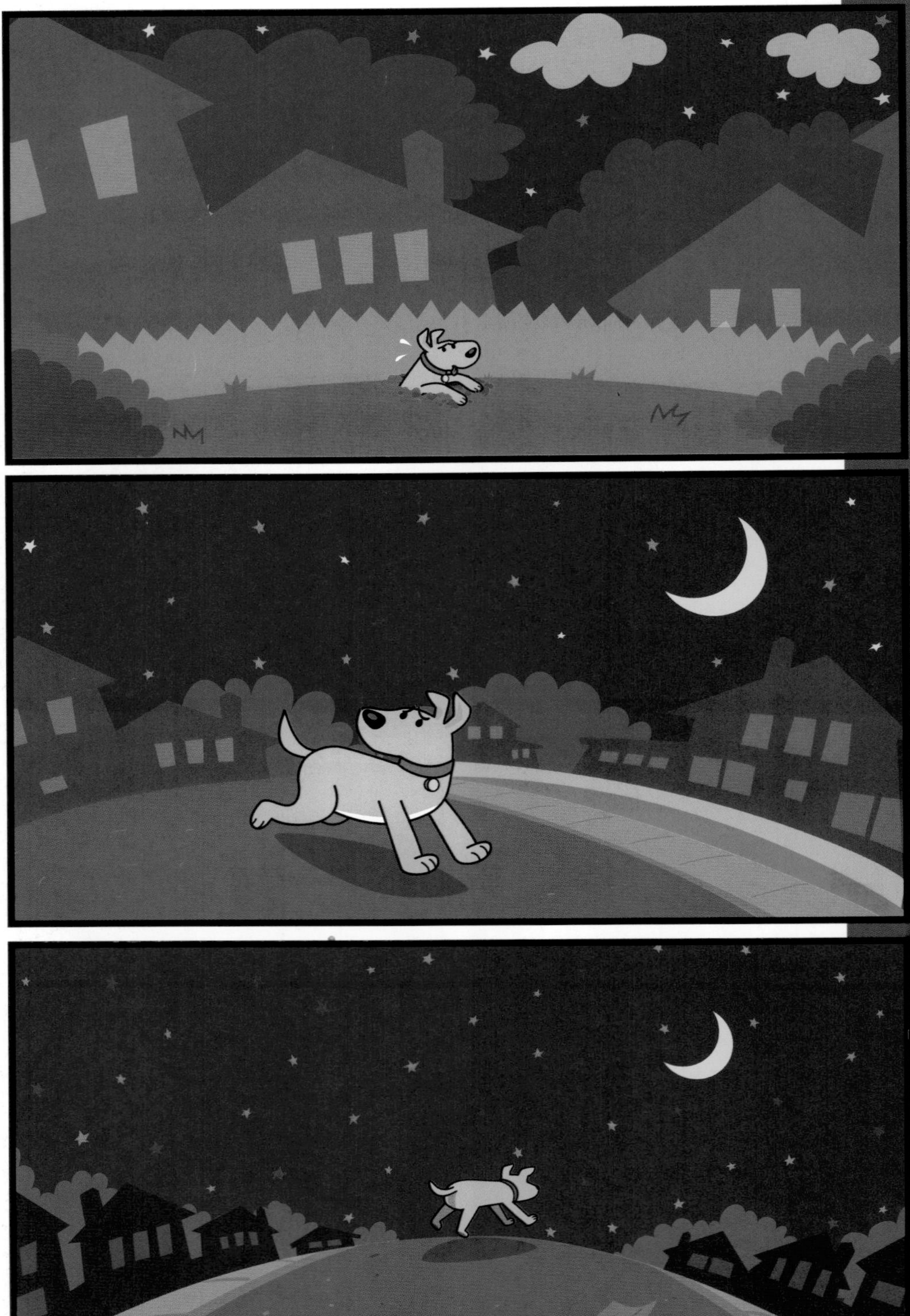

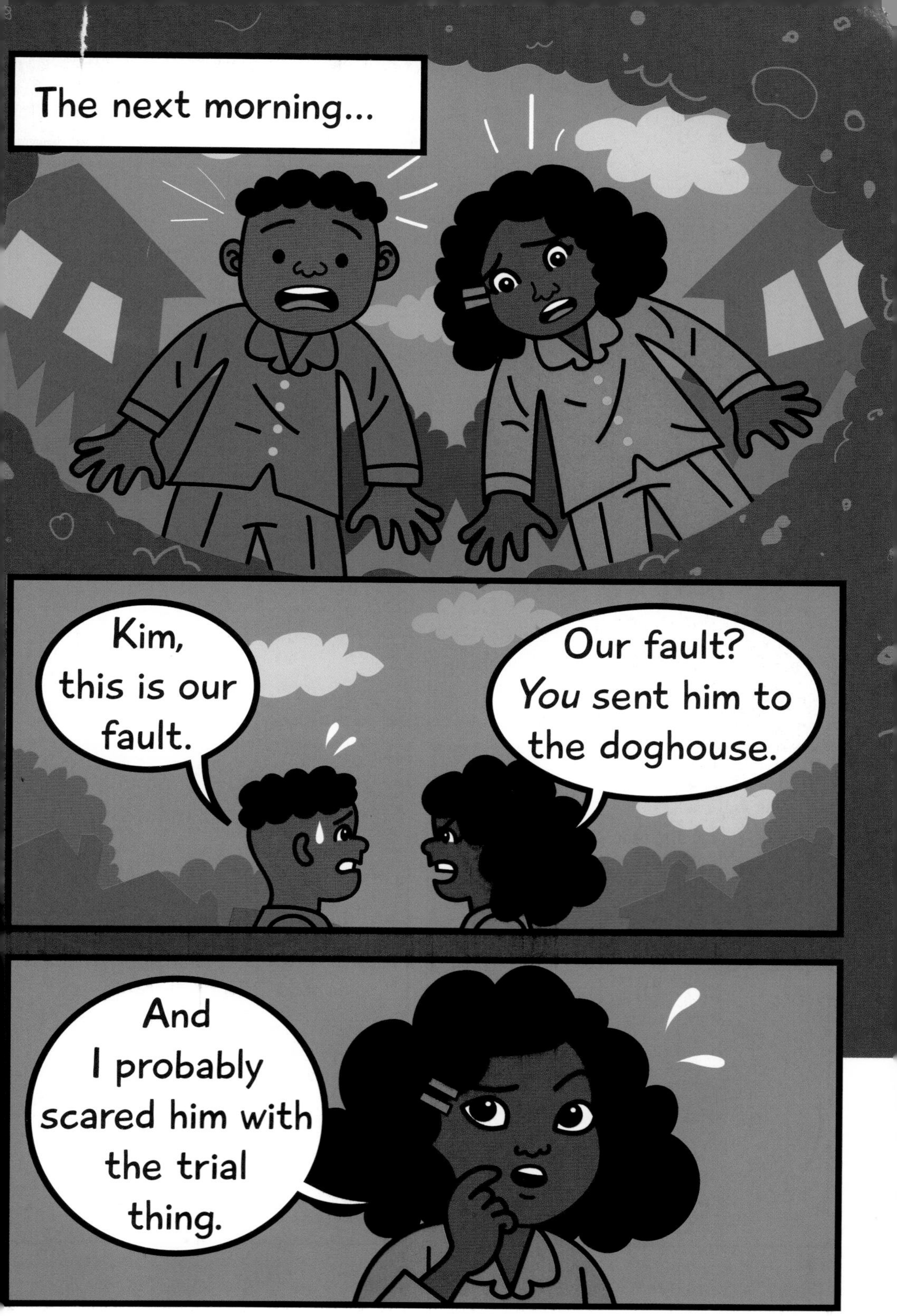

The next morning...
Kim, this is our fault.
Our fault? *You* sent him to the doghouse.
And I probably scared him with the trial thing.

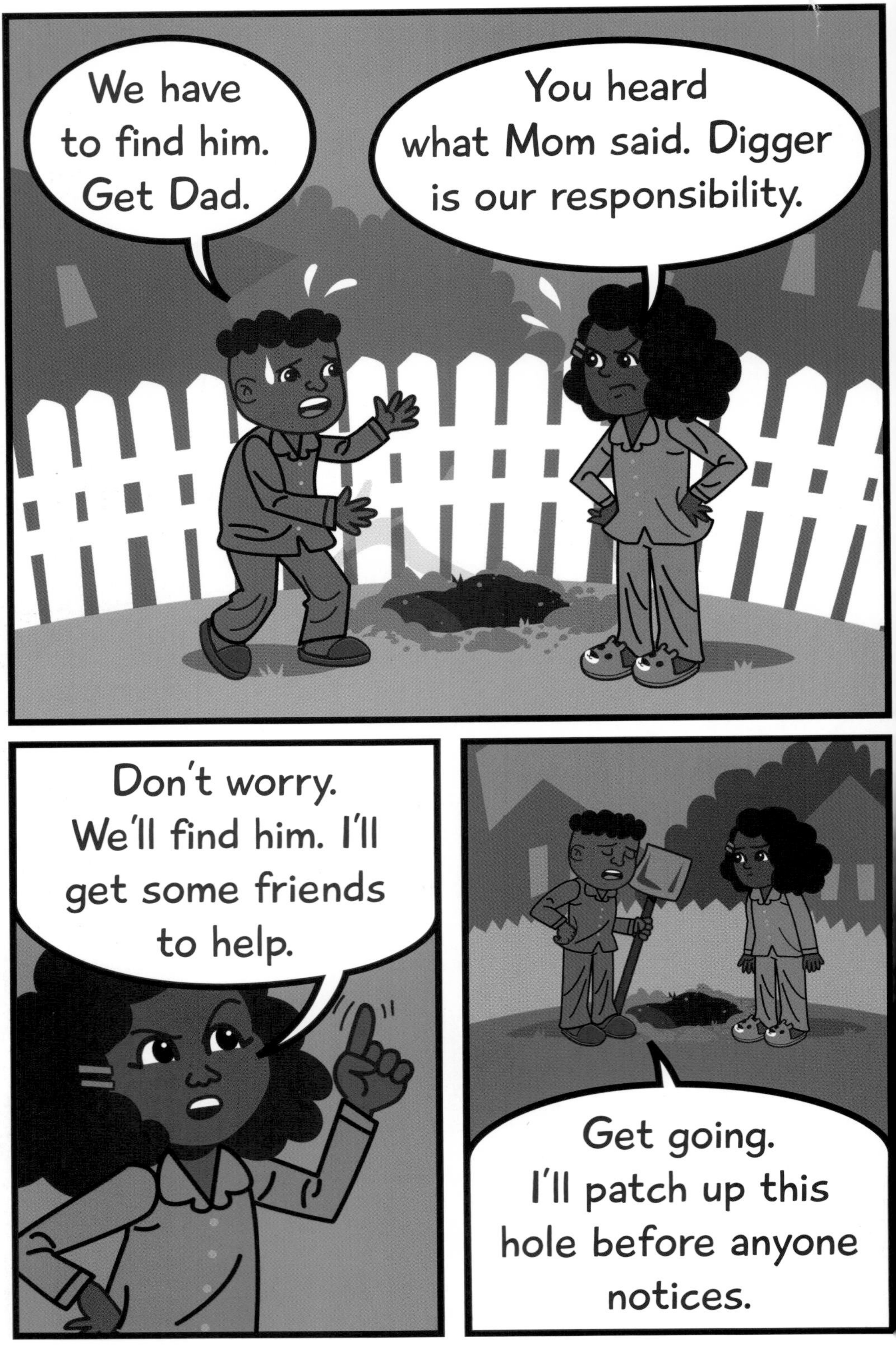
We have to find him. Get Dad.
You heard what Mom said. Digger is our responsibility.
Don't worry. We'll find him. I'll get some friends to help.
Get going. I'll patch up this hole before anyone notices.

Kim and her friends search Fairville, one street after the other...

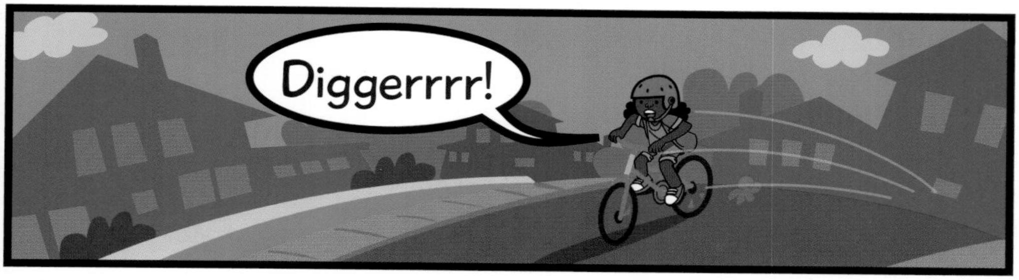
Diggerrrr!

from the school to the shopping mall...

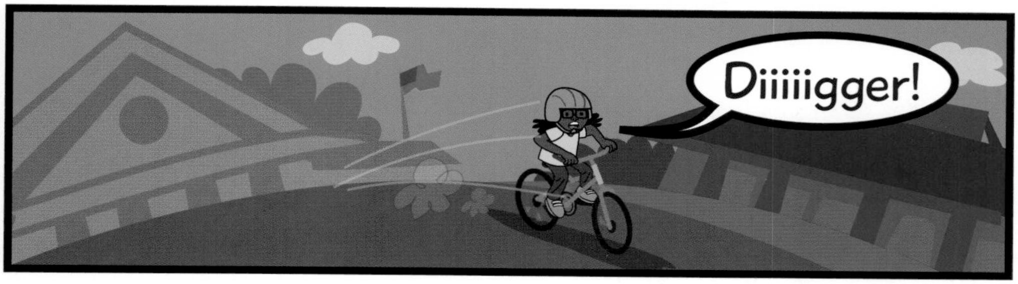
Diiiiigger!

past the church and the courthouse...

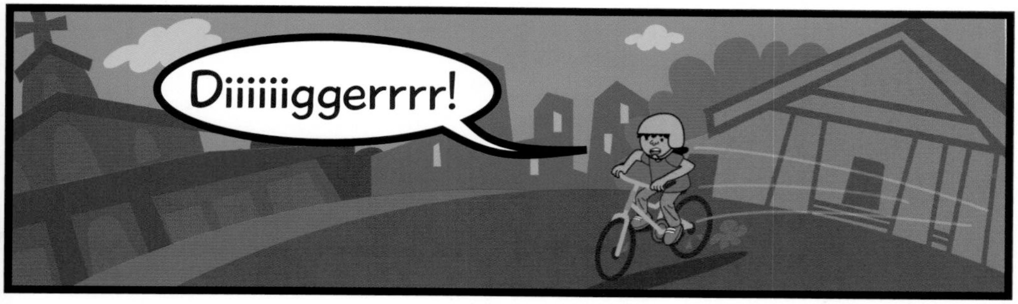
Diiiiiiggerrrr!

beyond the farms, all the way to the edge of town.

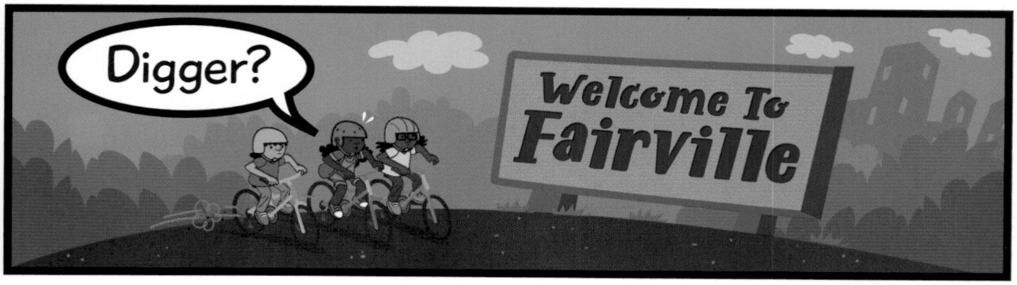
Digger?
Welcome To Fairville

Miles and Miguel stop at Neil's house to ask for help.

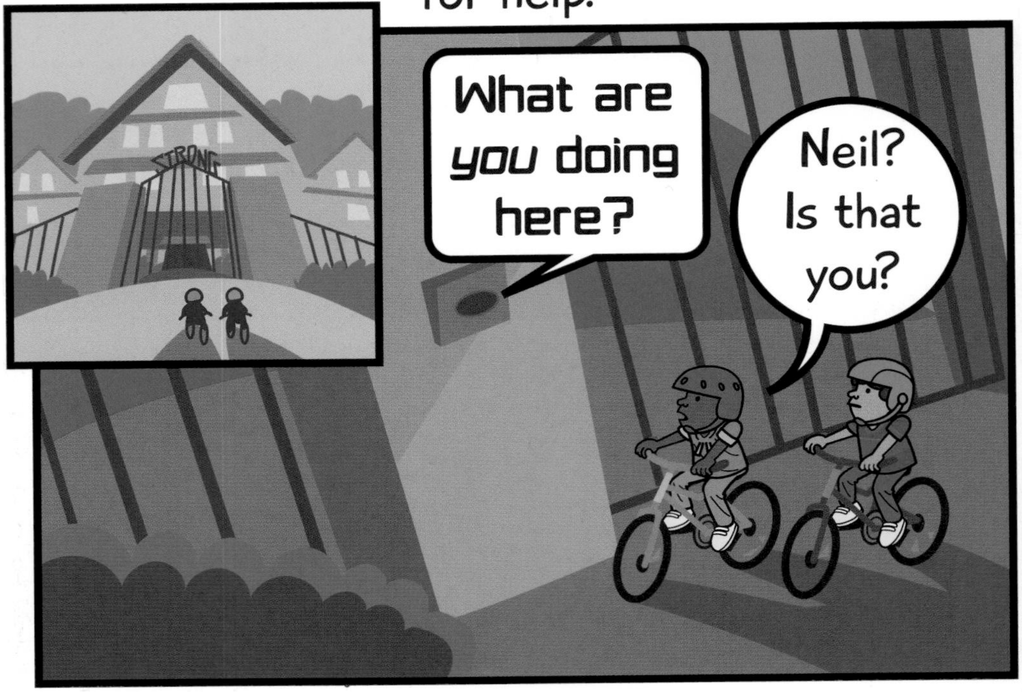
STRONG
What are *you* doing here?
Neil? Is that you?

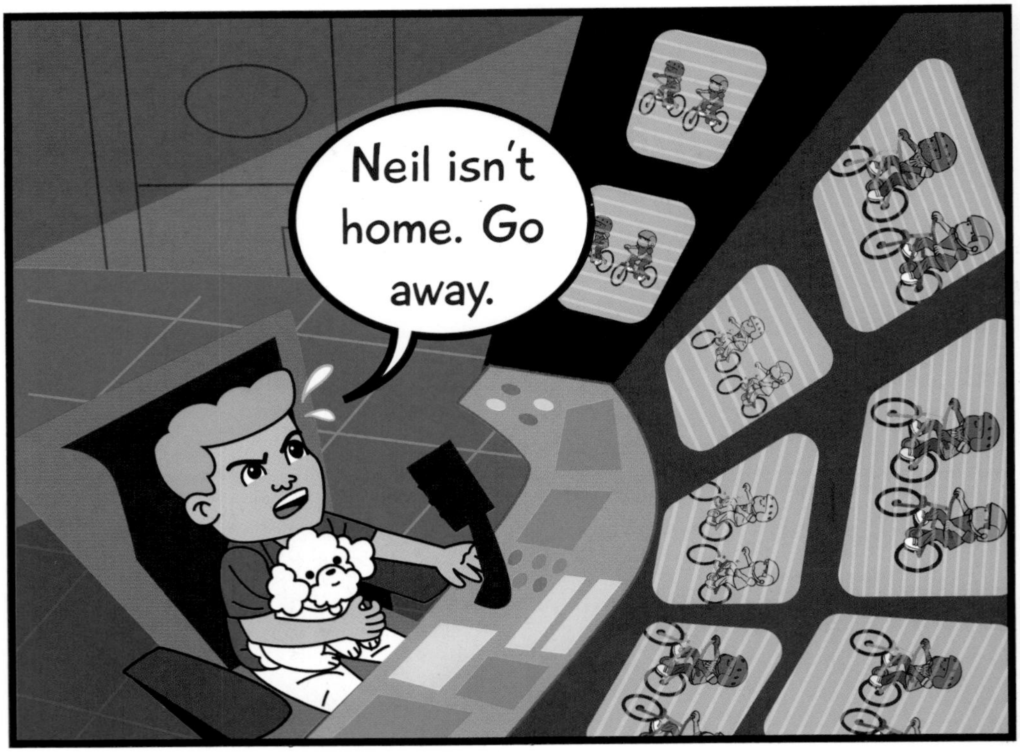
Neil isn't home. Go away.

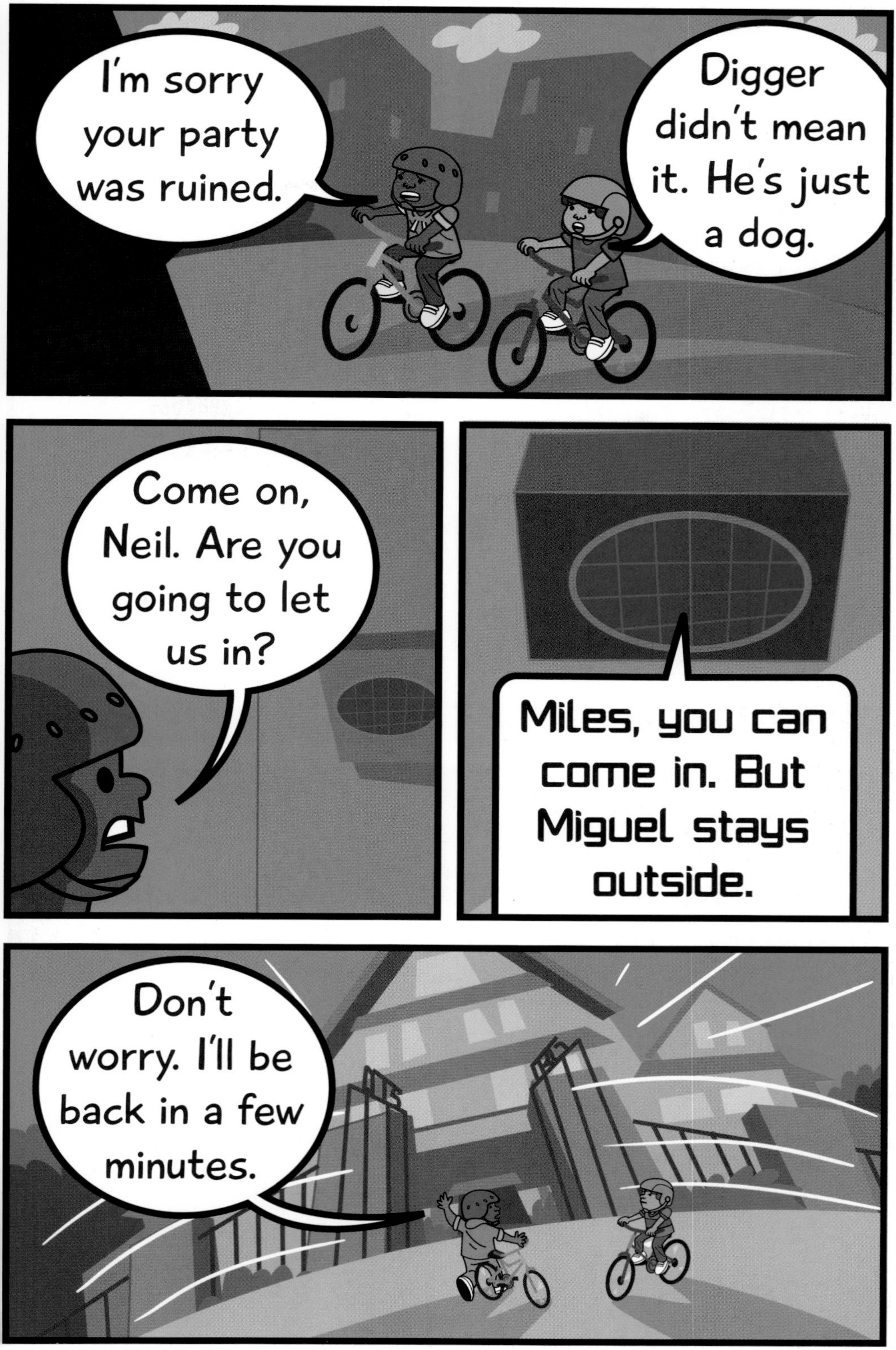

I'm sorry your party was ruined.
Digger didn't mean it. He's just a dog.
Come on, Neil. Are you going to let us in?
Miles, you can come in. But Miguel stays outside.
Don't worry. I'll be back in a few minutes.

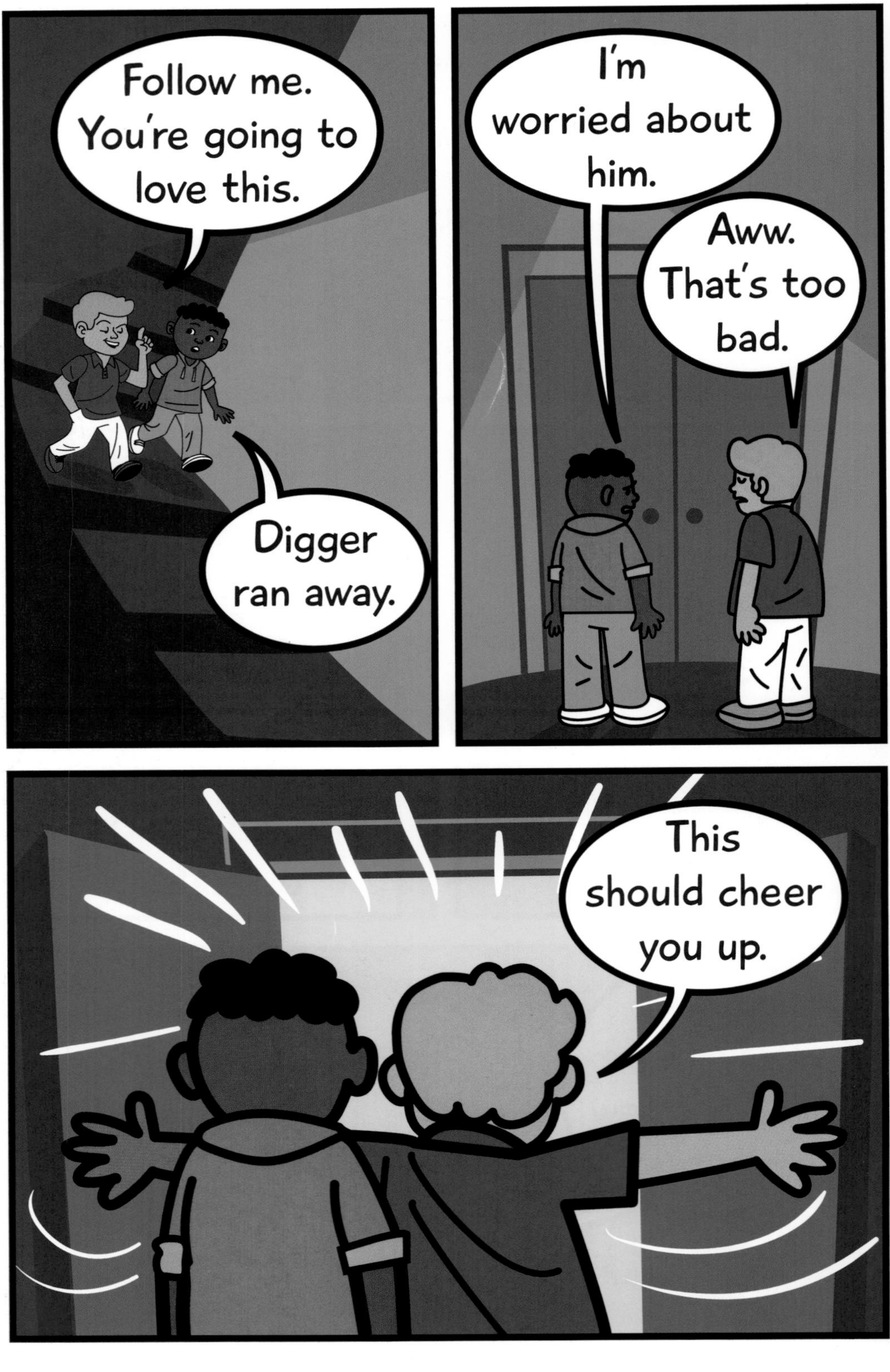
Follow me. You're going to love this.
Digger ran away.
I'm worried about him.
Aww. That's too bad.
This should cheer you up.

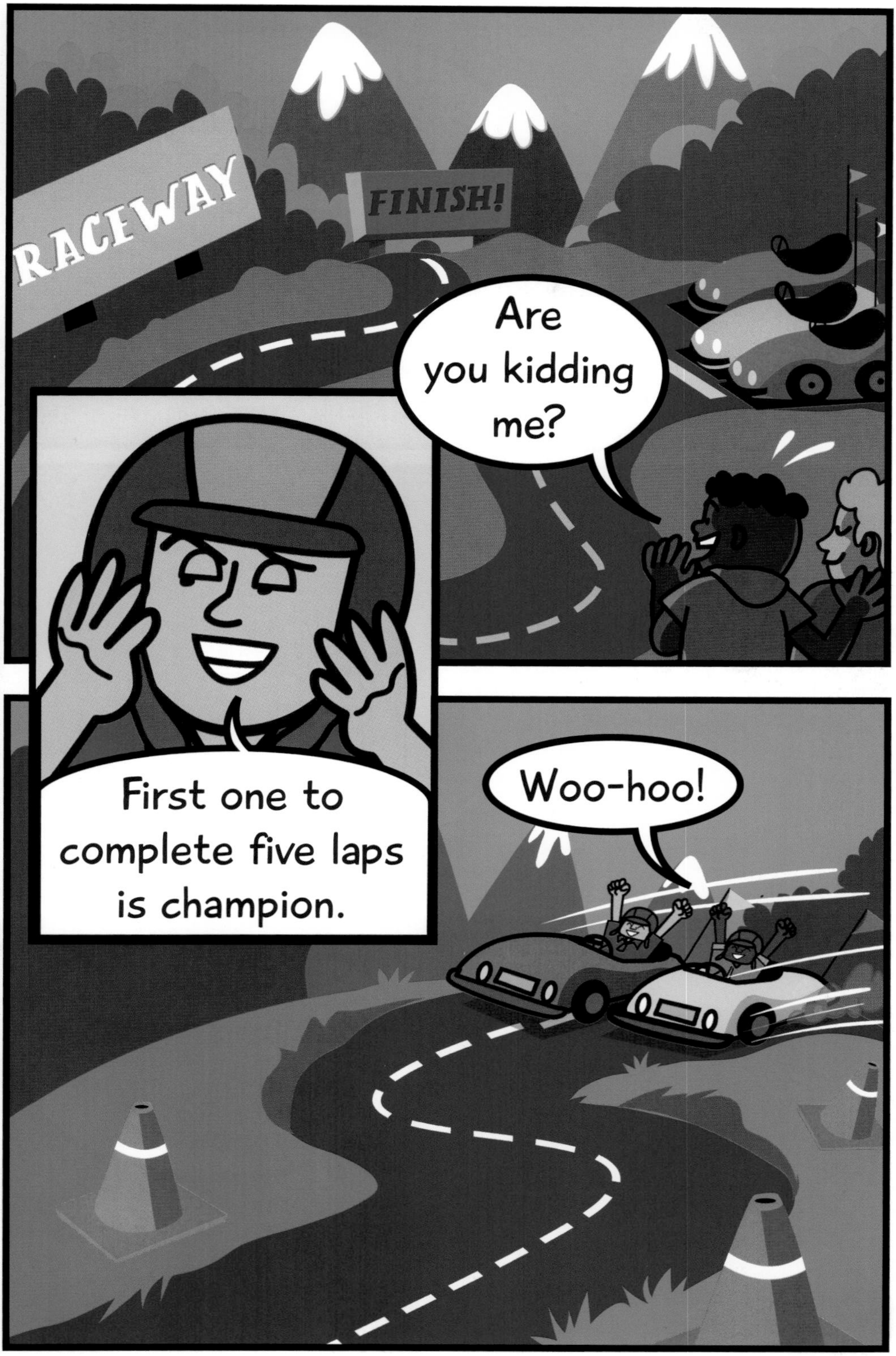
RACEWAY
FINISH!
Are you kidding me?
First one to complete five laps is champion.
Woo-hoo!

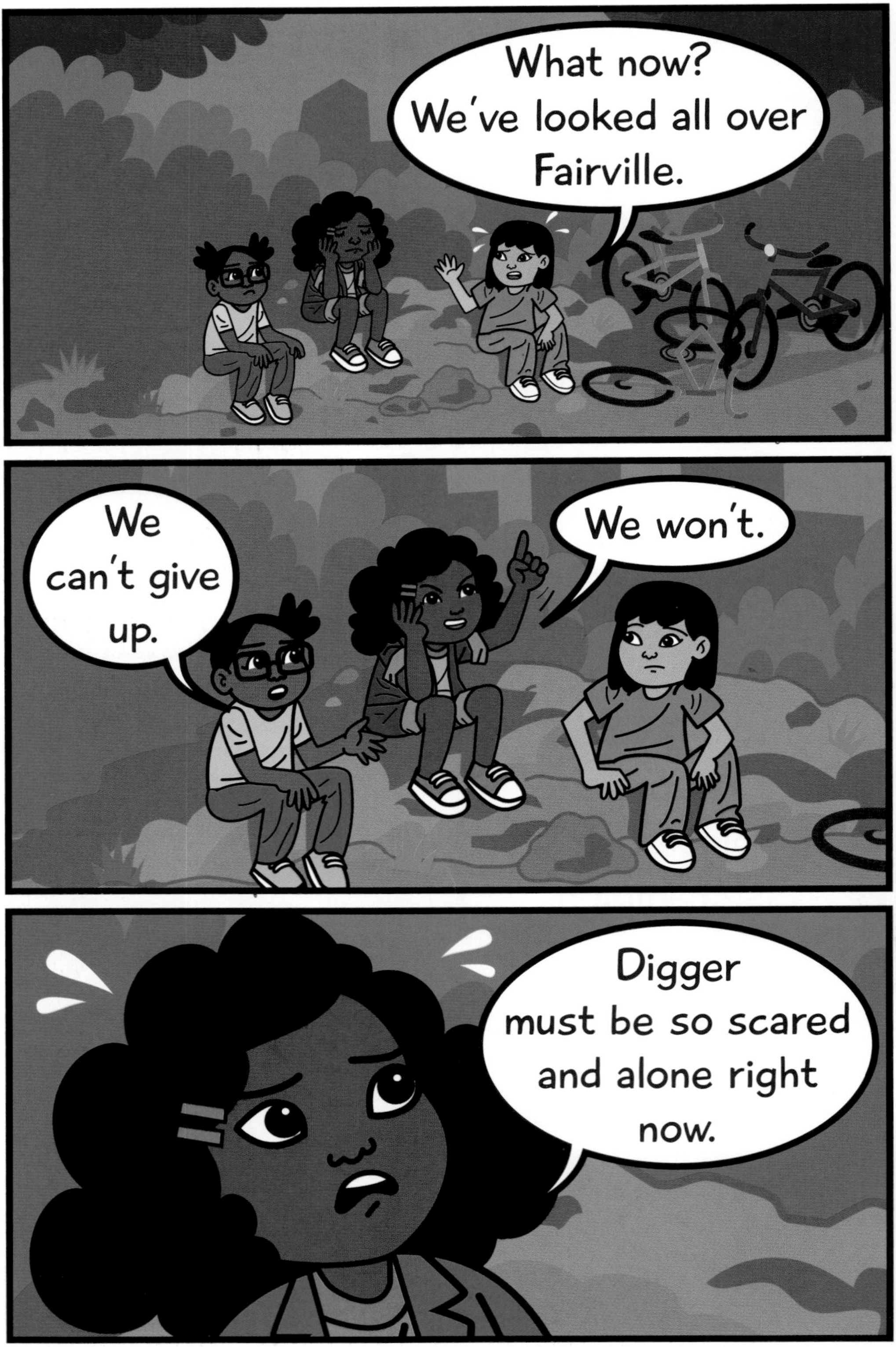
What now? We've looked all over Fairville.
We can't give up.
We won't.
Digger must be so scared and alone right now.

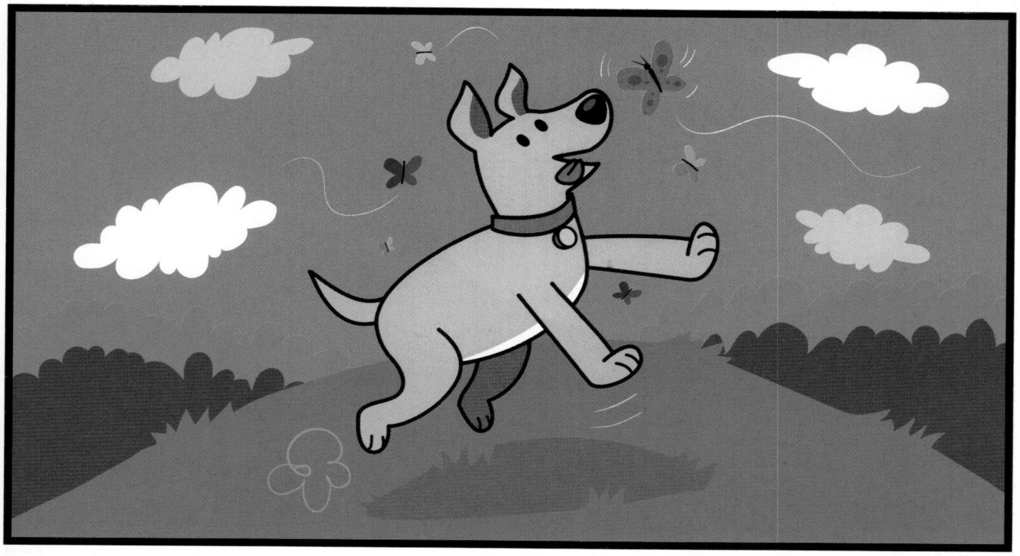

It looks like Digger is enjoying a little adventure away from home.

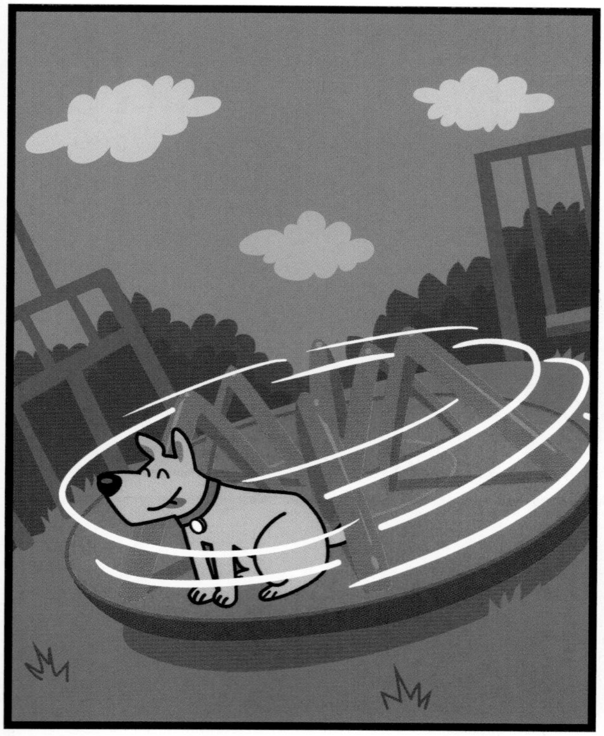

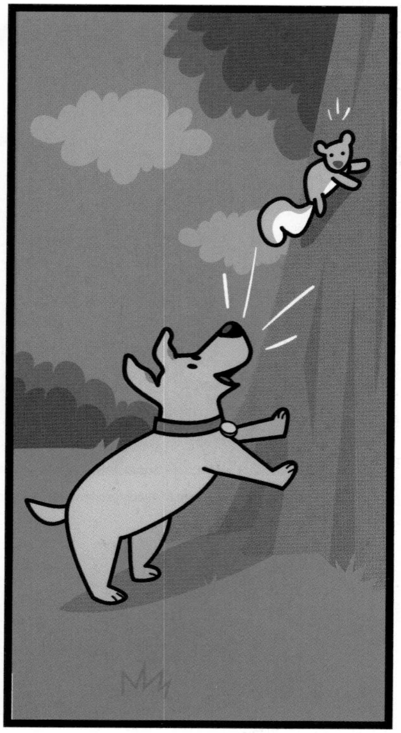

Digger thinks the playground and chasing squirrels is a lot more fun than the Kids' Court.

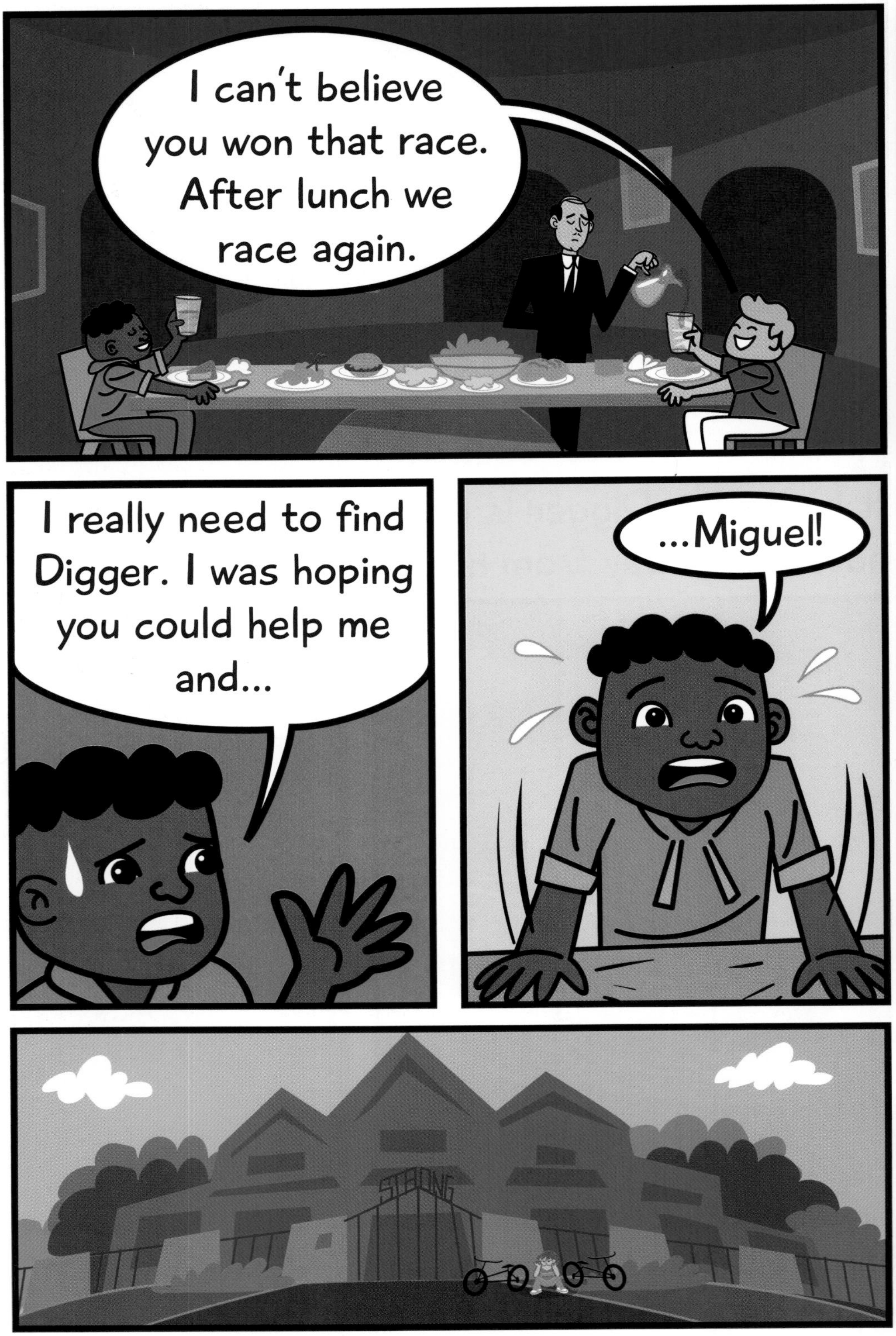
I can't believe you won that race. After lunch we race again.
I really need to find Digger. I was hoping you could help me and...
...Miguel!

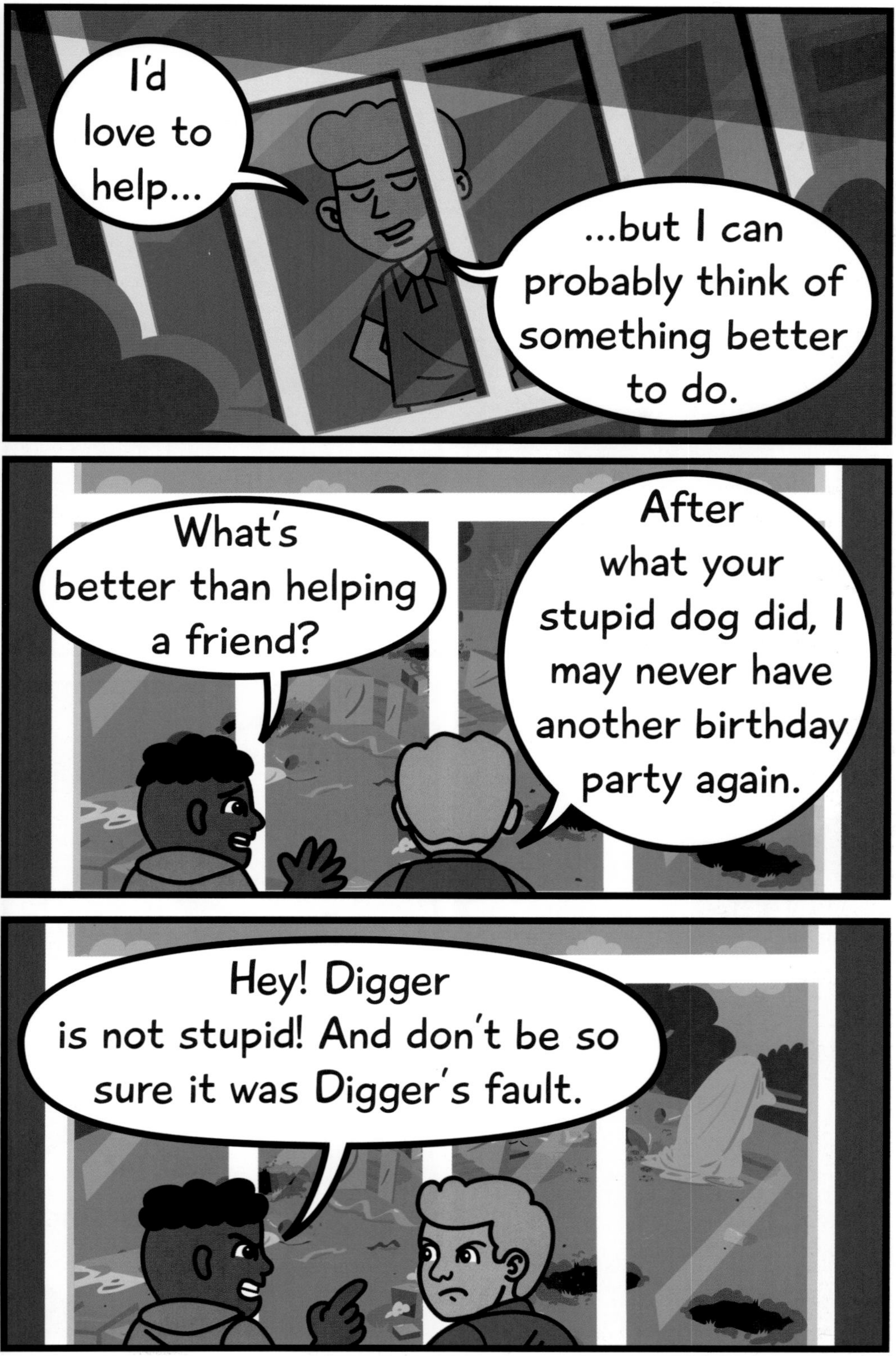
I'd love to help...
...but I can probably think of something better to do.
What's better than helping a friend?
After what your stupid dog did, I may never have another birthday party again.
Hey! Digger is not stupid! And don't be so sure it was Digger's fault.

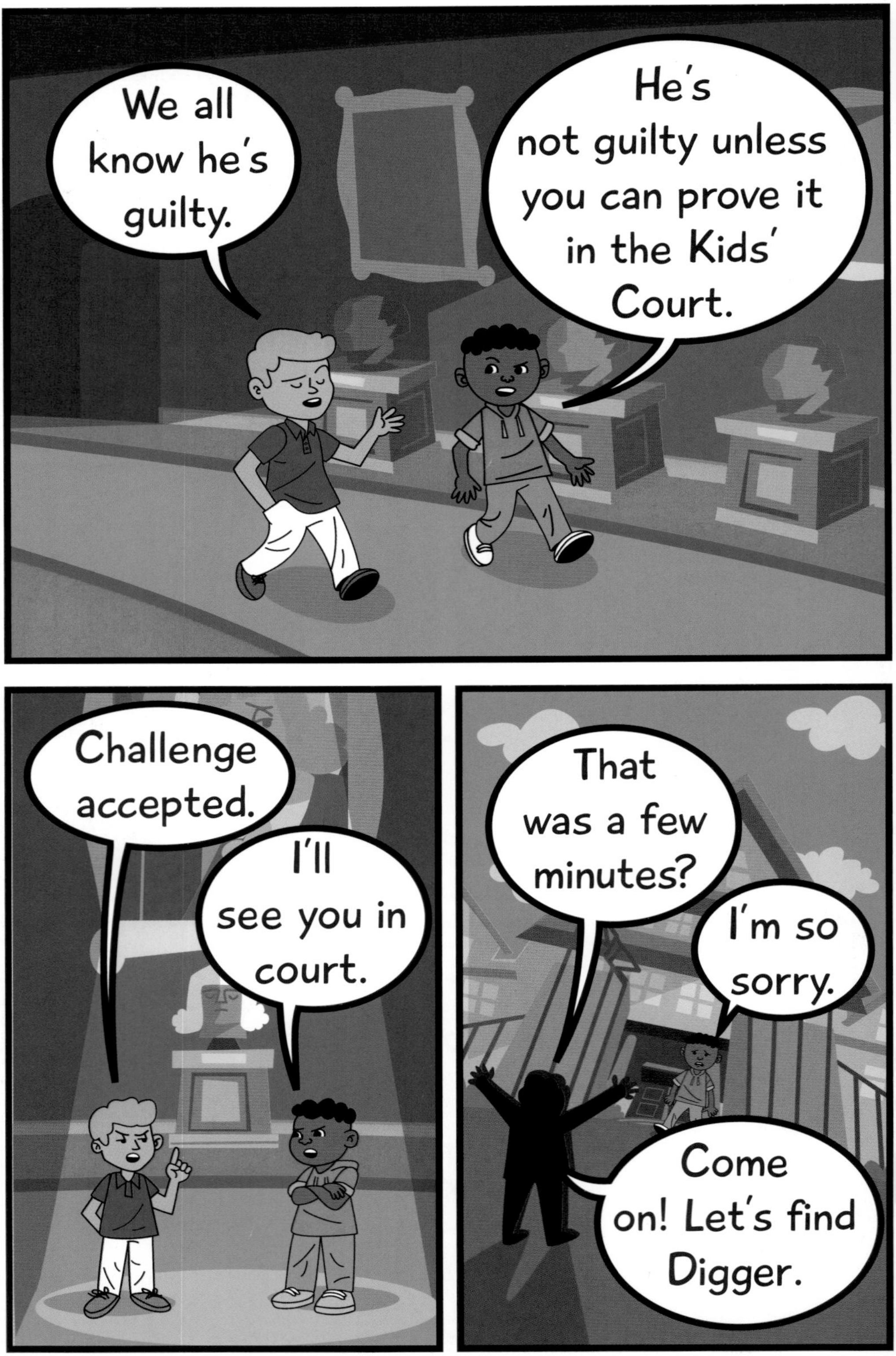
We all know he's guilty.
He's not guilty unless you can prove it in the Kids' Court.
Challenge accepted.
I'll see you in court.
That was a few minutes?
I'm so sorry.
Come on! Let's find Digger.

After a long day of searching...

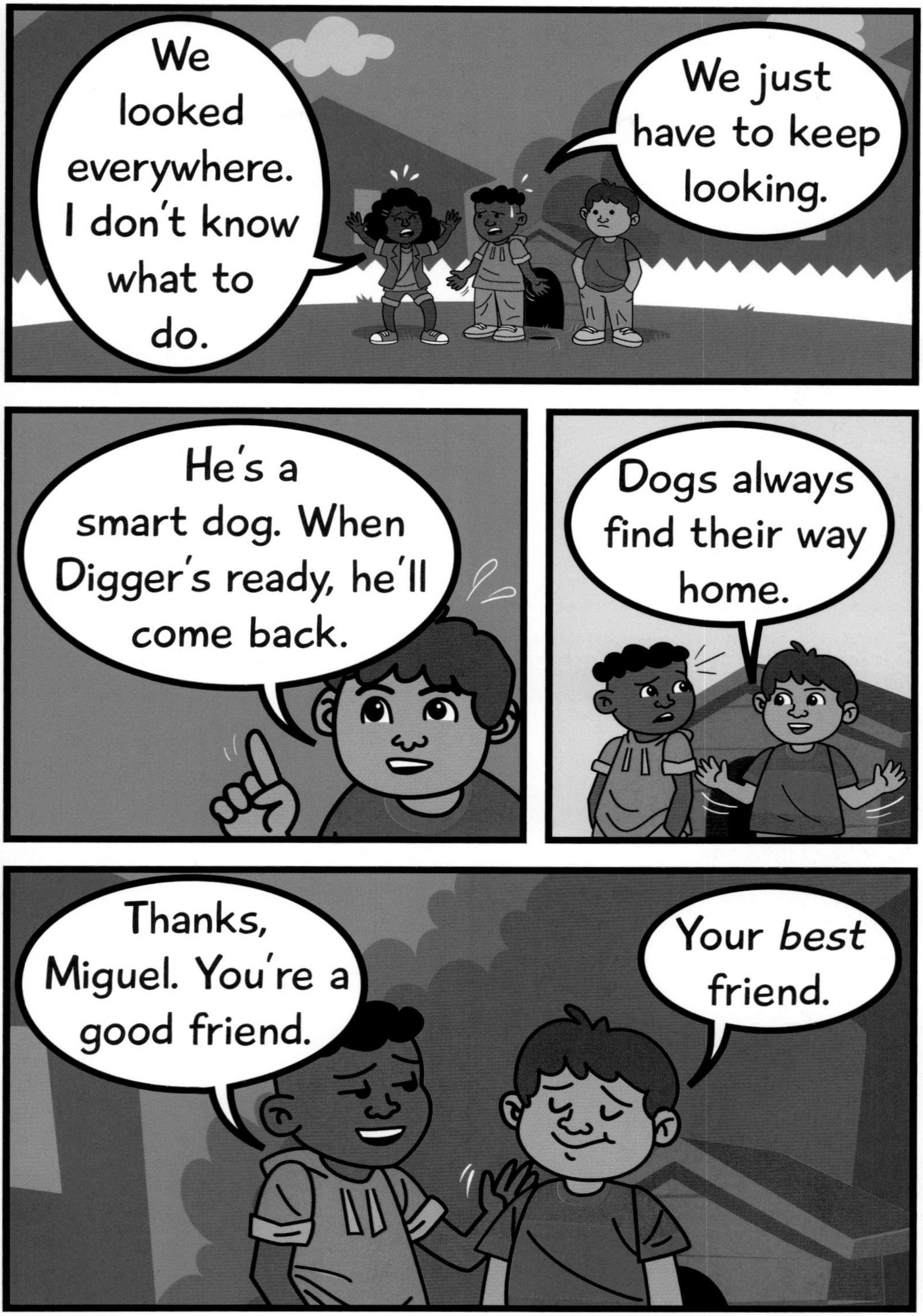
We looked everywhere. I don't know what to do.
We just have to keep looking.
He's a smart dog. When Digger's ready, he'll come back.
Dogs always find their way home.
Thanks, Miguel. You're a good friend.
Your *best* friend.

A little adventure is always fun...

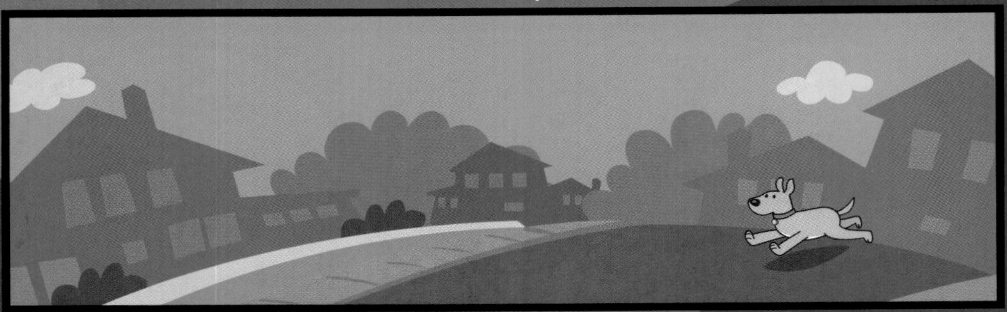

...but back to Fairville, Digger goes.

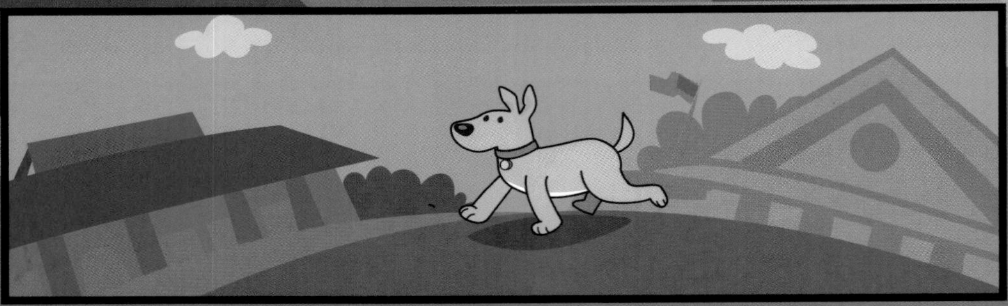

Because even a dog knows...

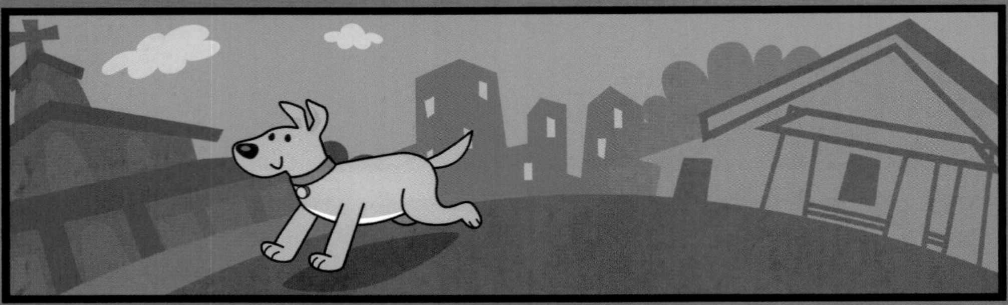

...you can't run away from your problems.

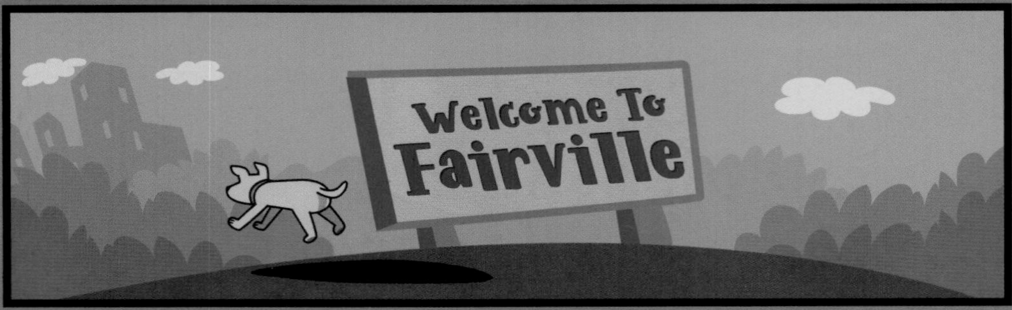
Welcome To
Fairville

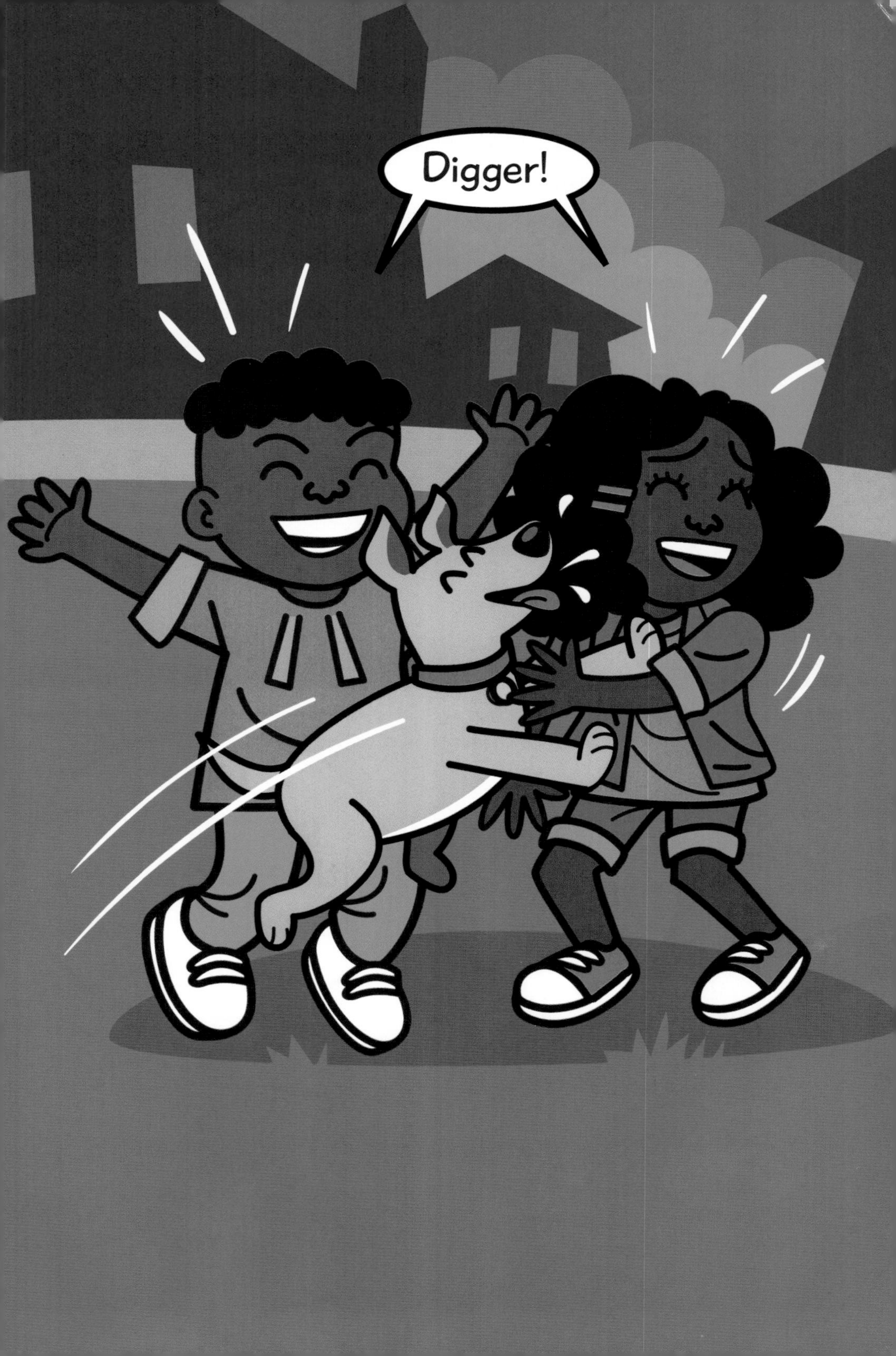
Digger!

At last, a dog will have his day in court.

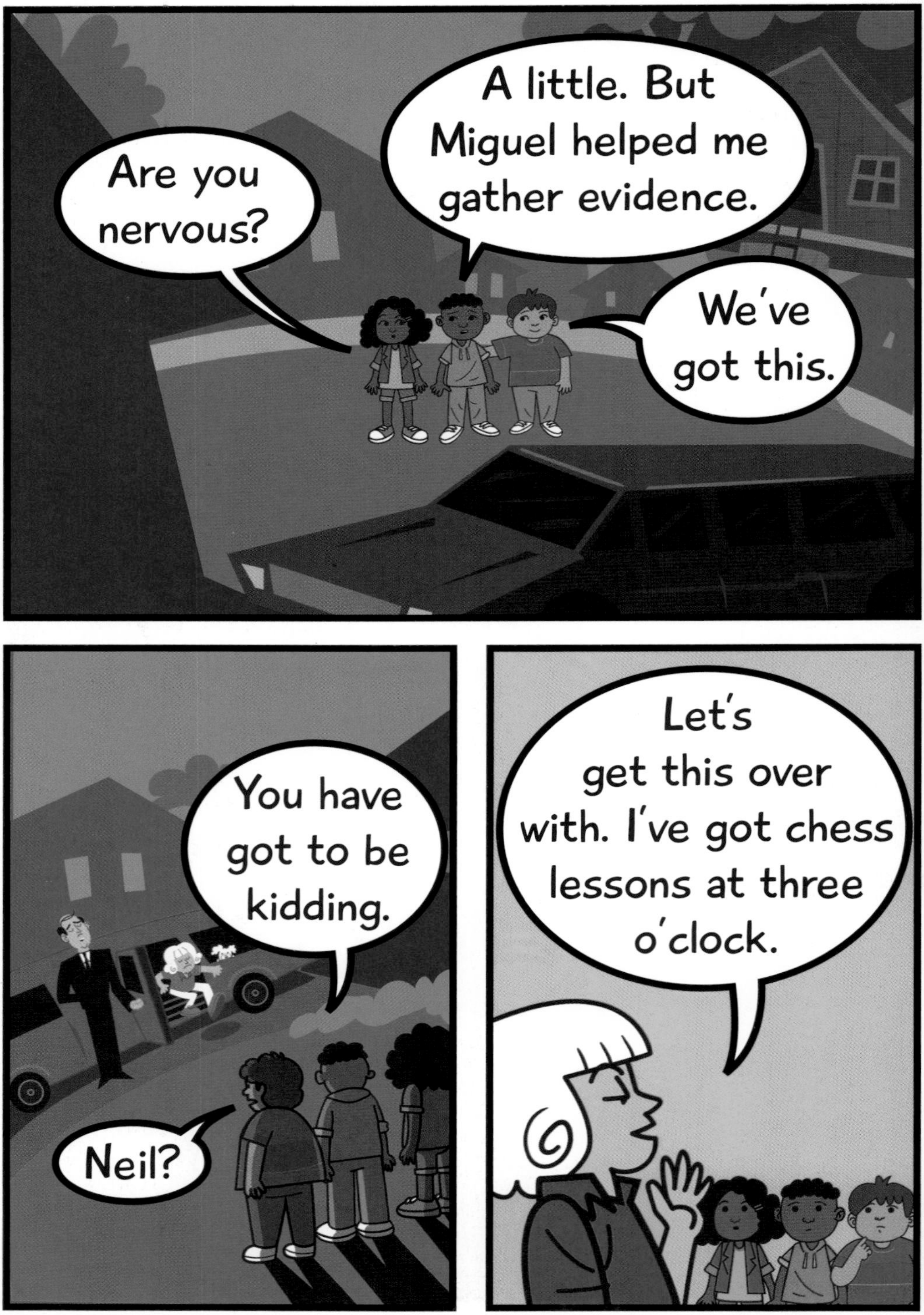
Are you nervous?
A little. But Miguel helped me gather evidence.
We've got this.
You have got to be kidding.
Neil?
Let's get this over with. I've got chess lessons at three o'clock.

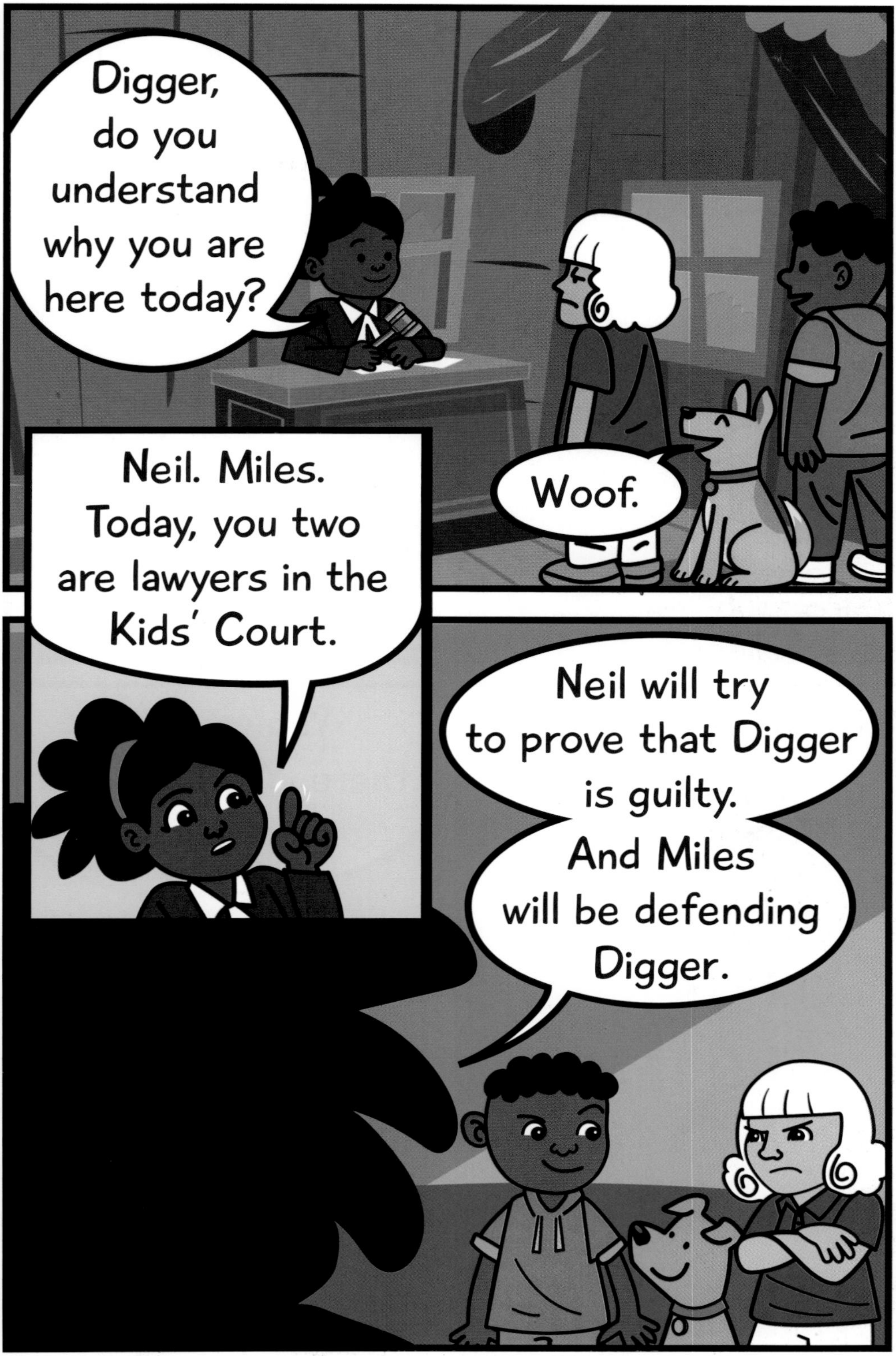
Digger, do you understand why you are here today?
Woof.
Neil. Miles. Today, you two are lawyers in the Kids' Court.
Neil will try to prove that Digger is guilty.
And Miles will be defending Digger.

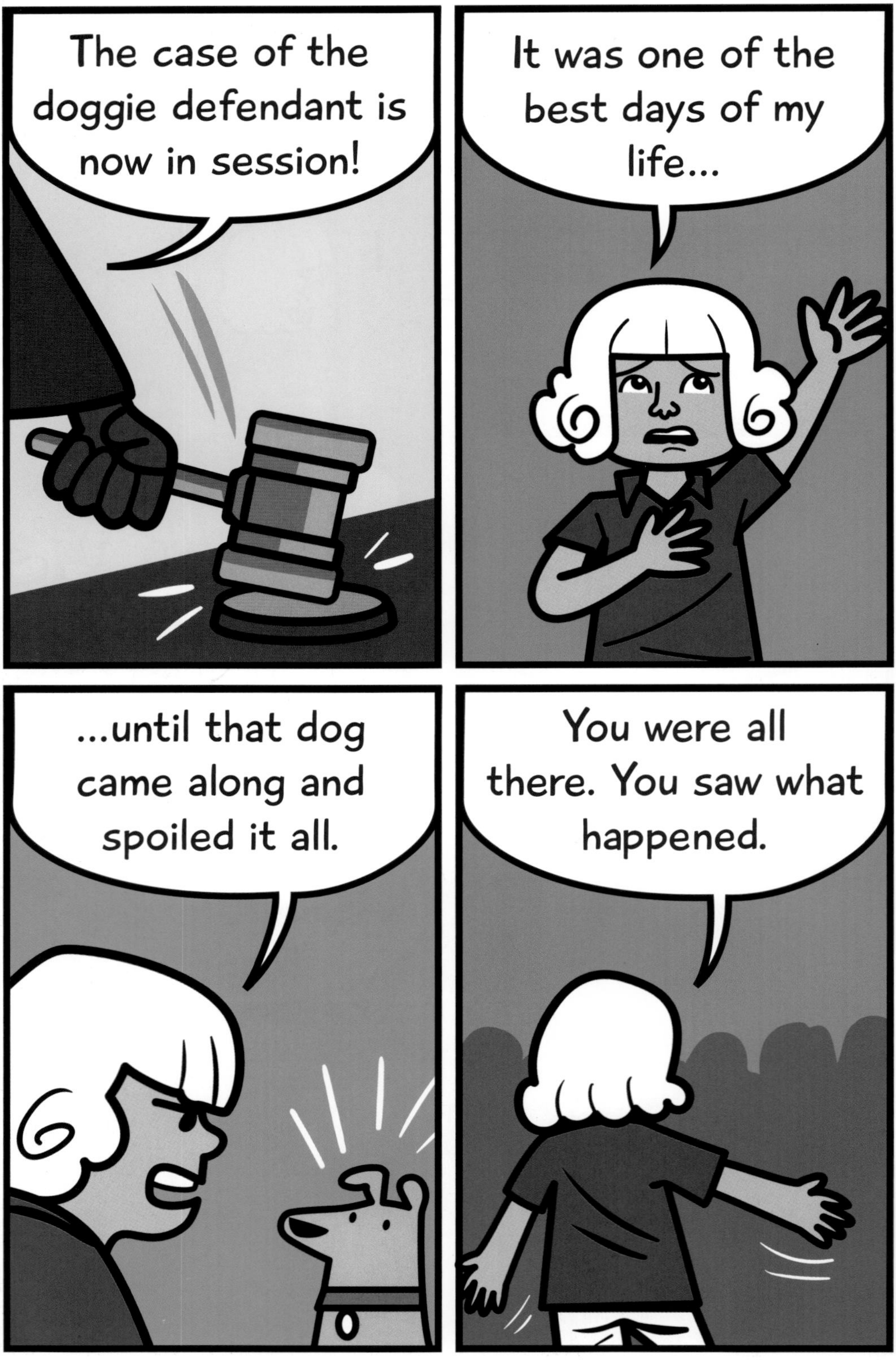
The case of the doggie defendant is now in session!
It was one of the best days of my life...
...until that dog came along and spoiled it all.
You were all there. You saw what happened.

Neil weaves a story of what he thinks happened that day...

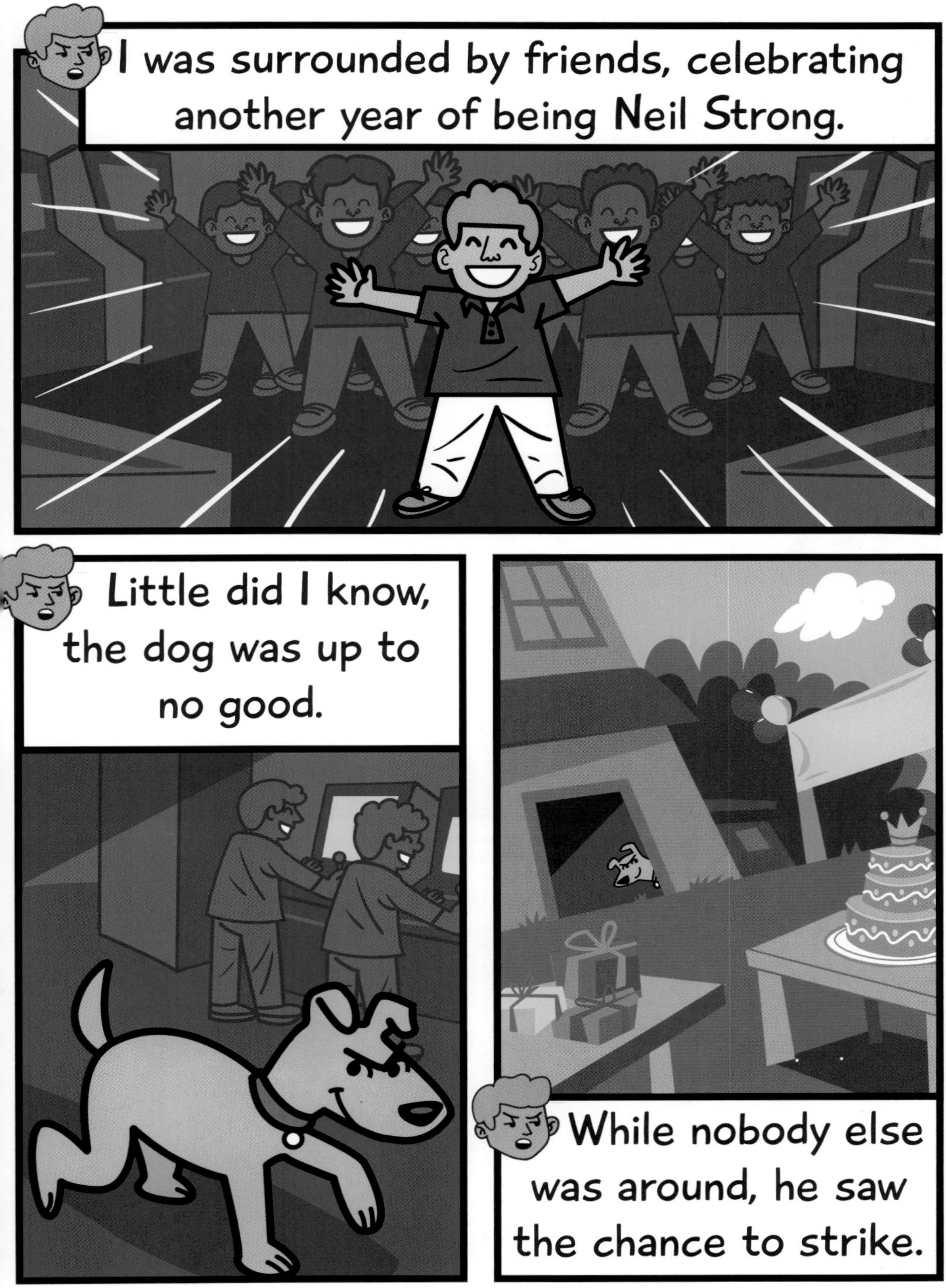

I was surrounded by friends, celebrating another year of being Neil Strong.
Little did I know, the dog was up to no good.
While nobody else was around, he saw the chance to strike.

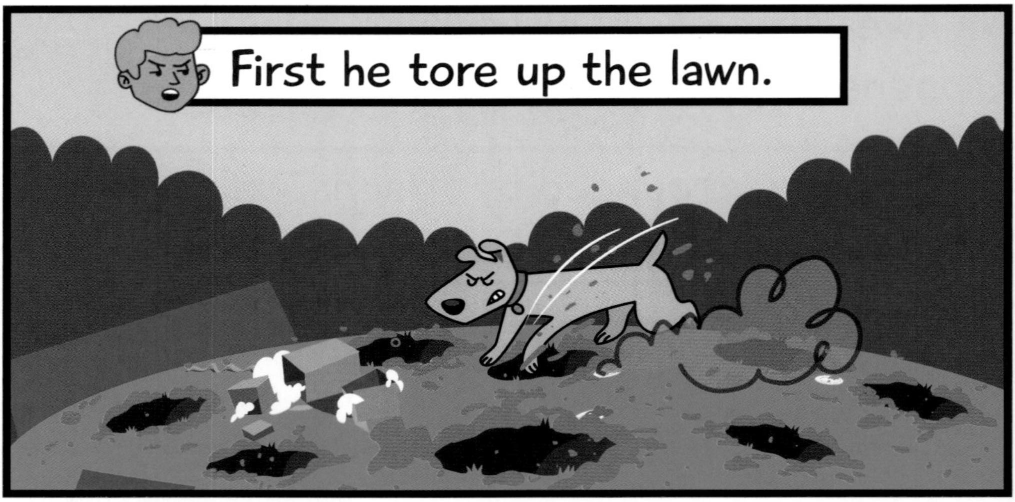
First he tore up the lawn.
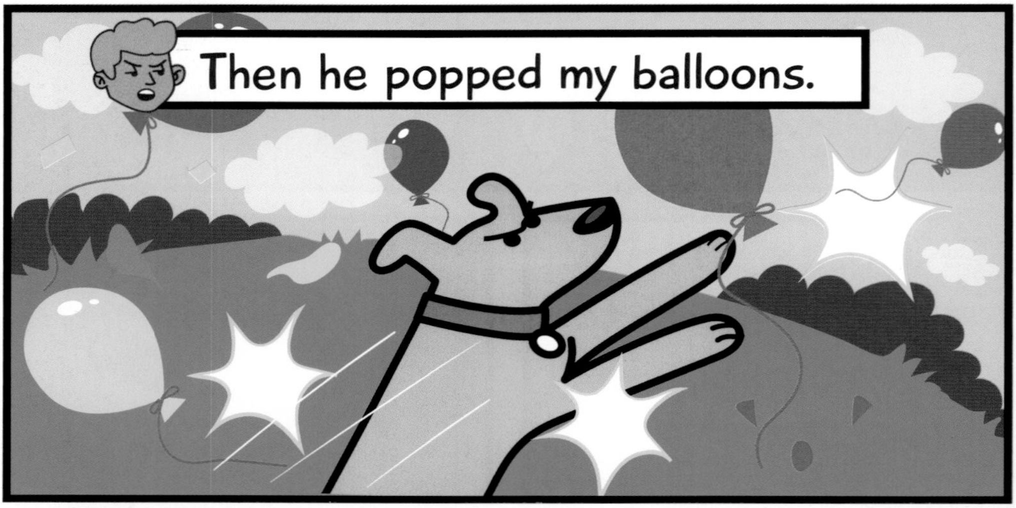
Then he popped my balloons.
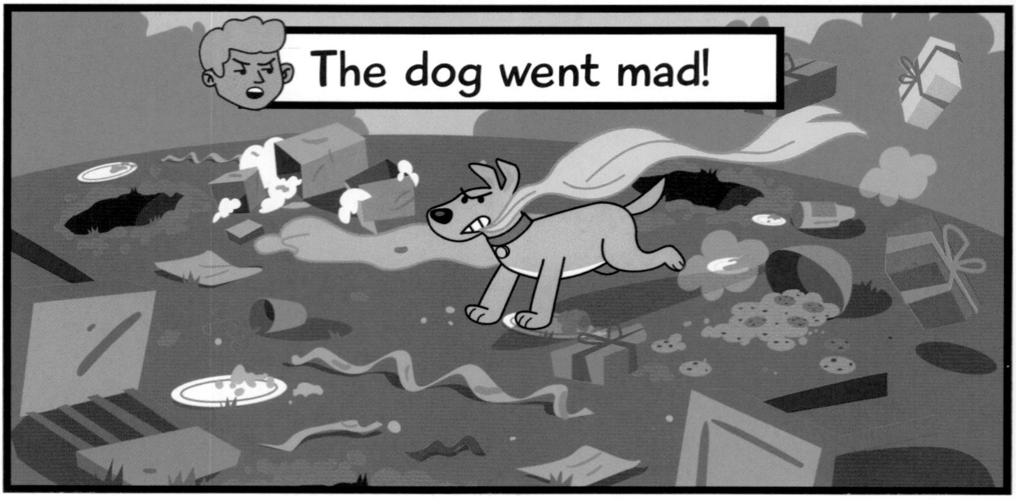
The dog went mad!

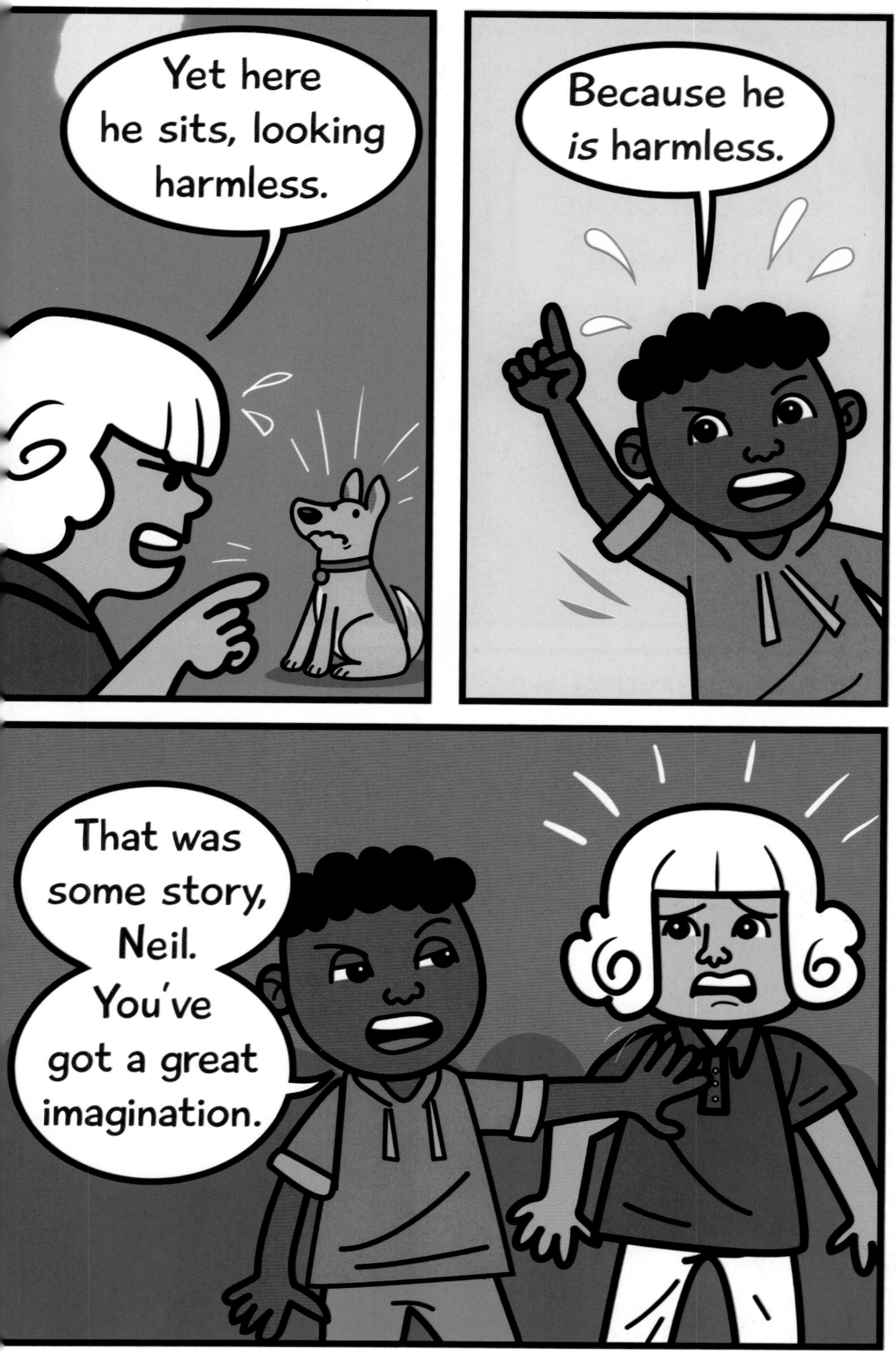
Yet here he *sits*, looking harmless.
Because he *is* harmless.
That was some story, Neil.
You've got a great imagination.

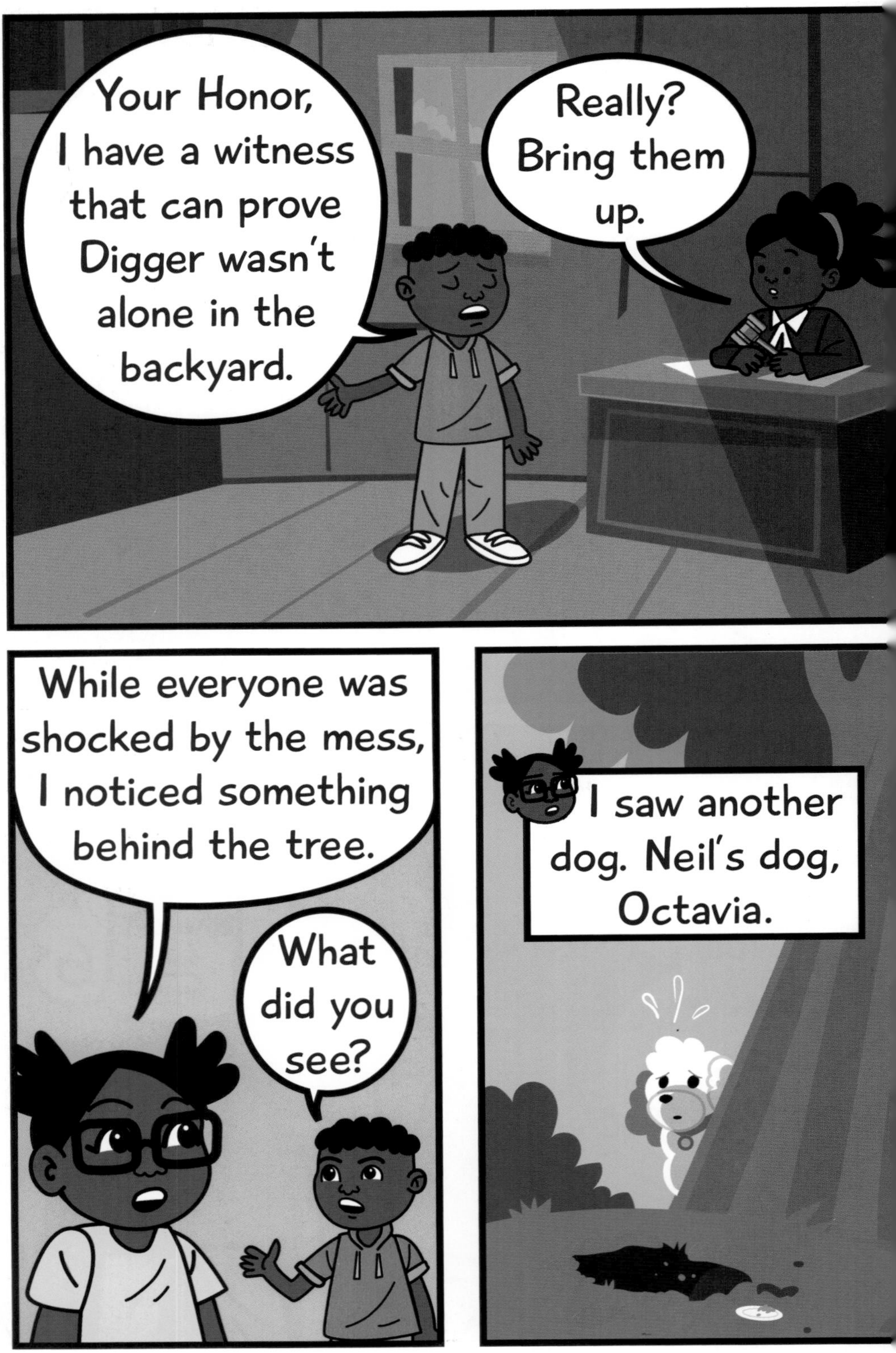
Your Honor, I have a witness that can prove Digger wasn't alone in the backyard.
Really? Bring them up.
While everyone was shocked by the mess, I noticed something behind the tree.
What did you see?
I saw another dog. Neil's dog, Octavia.

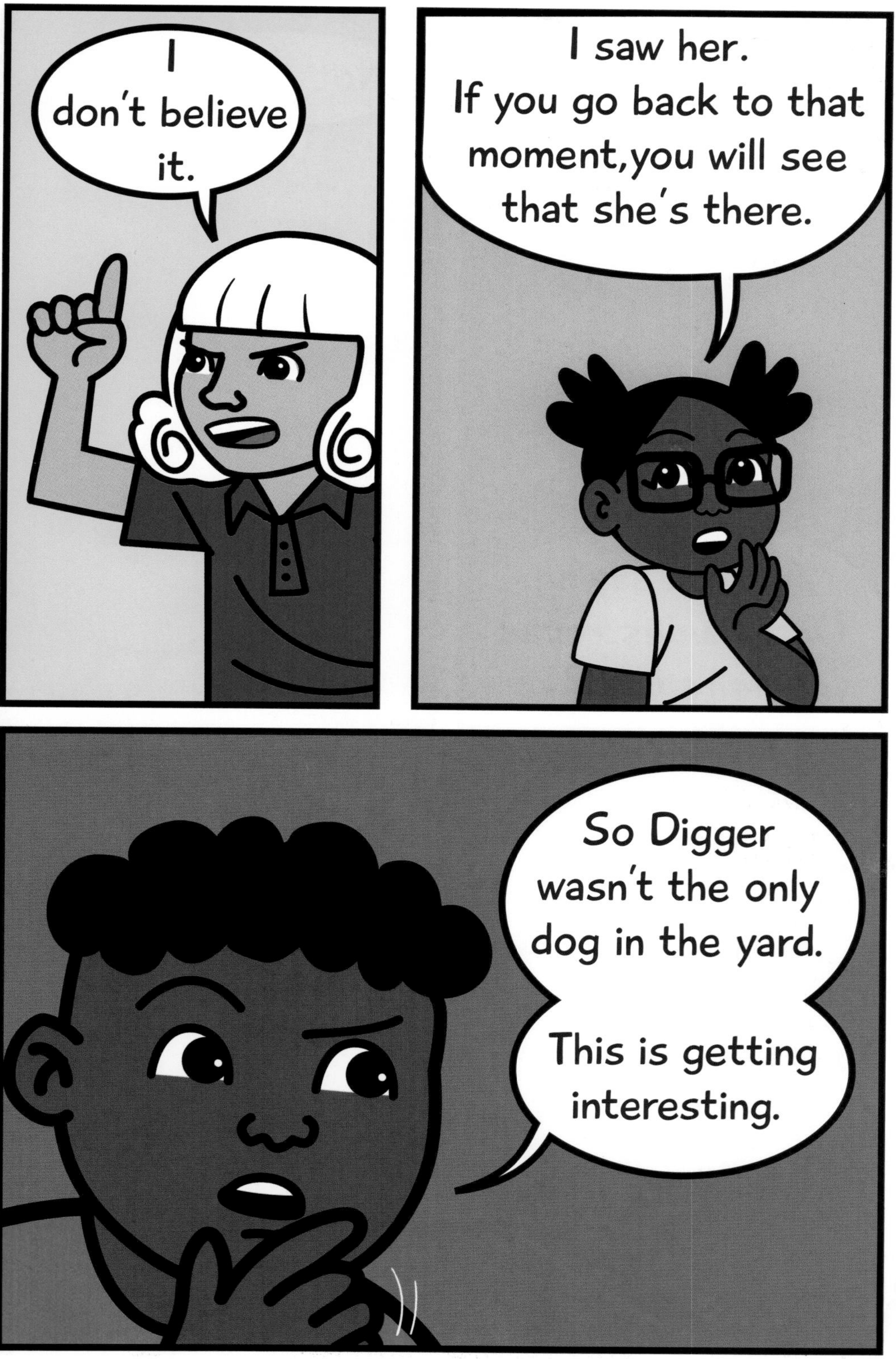
I don't believe it.
I saw her. If you go back to that moment,you will see that she's there.
So Digger wasn't the only dog in the yard.
This is getting interesting.

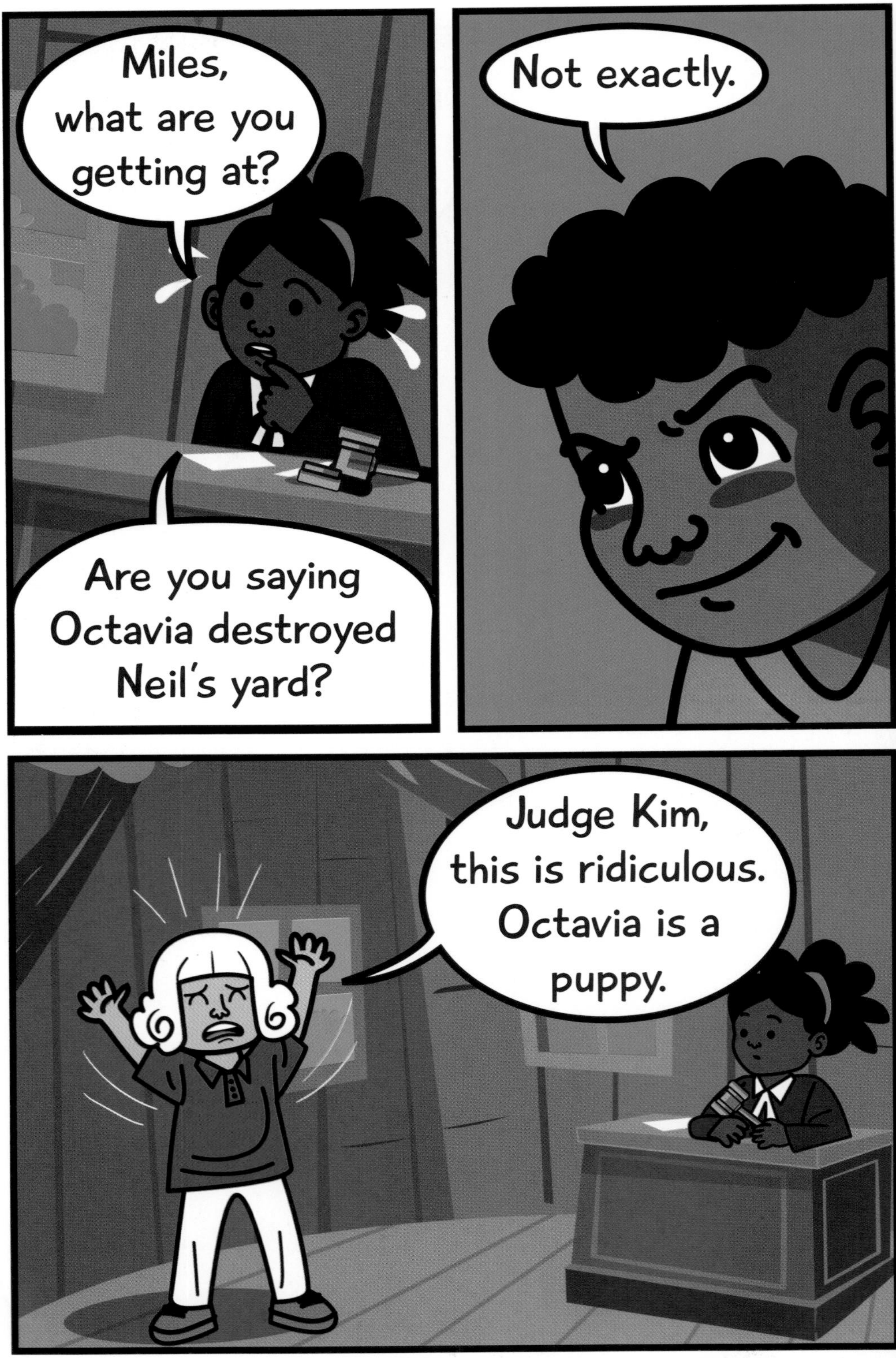
Miles, what are you getting at?
Are you saying Octavia destroyed Neil's yard?
Not exactly.
Judge Kim, this is ridiculous. Octavia is a puppy.

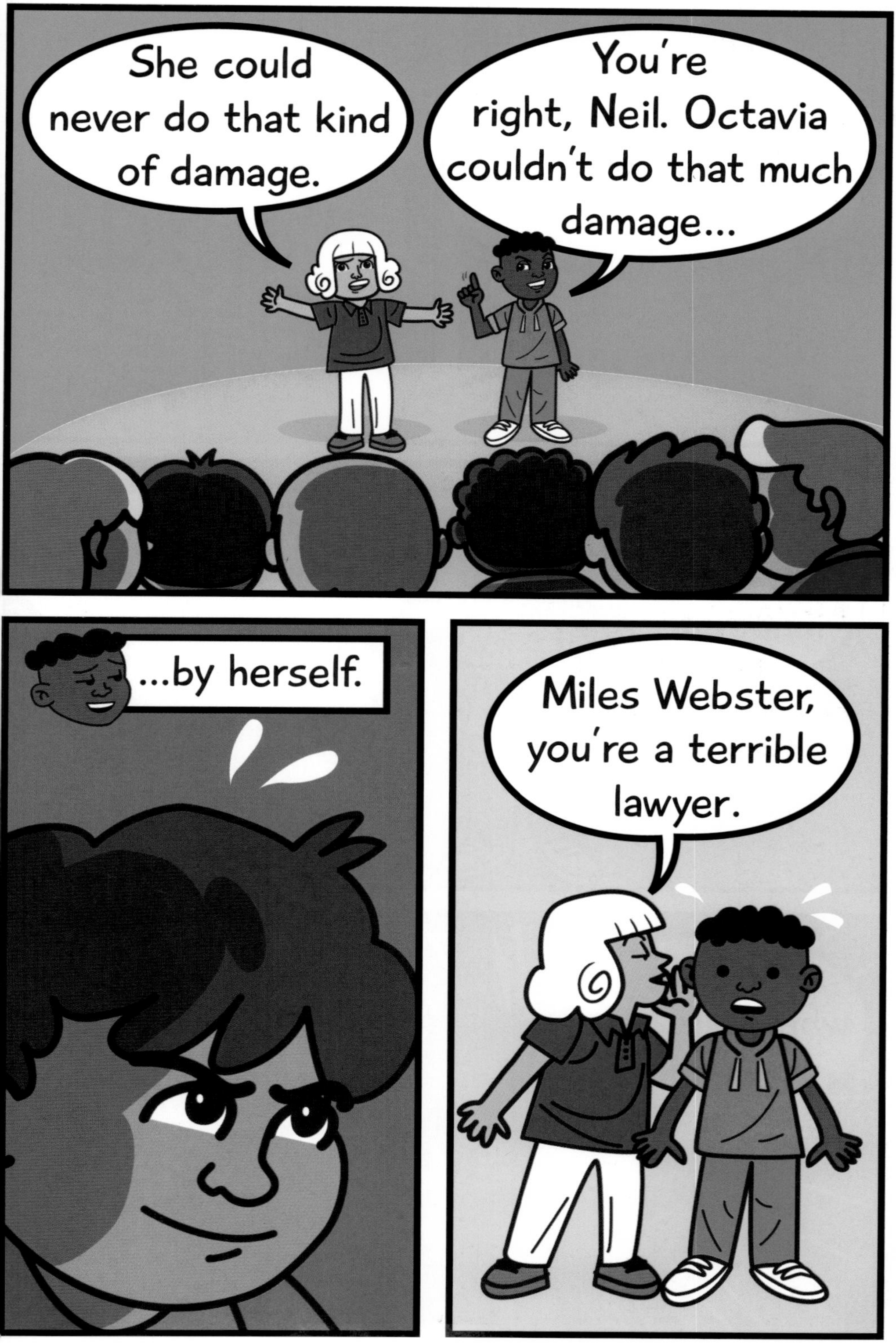
She could never do that kind of damage.
You're right, Neil. Octavia couldn't do that much damage...
...by herself.
Miles Webster, you're a terrible lawyer.

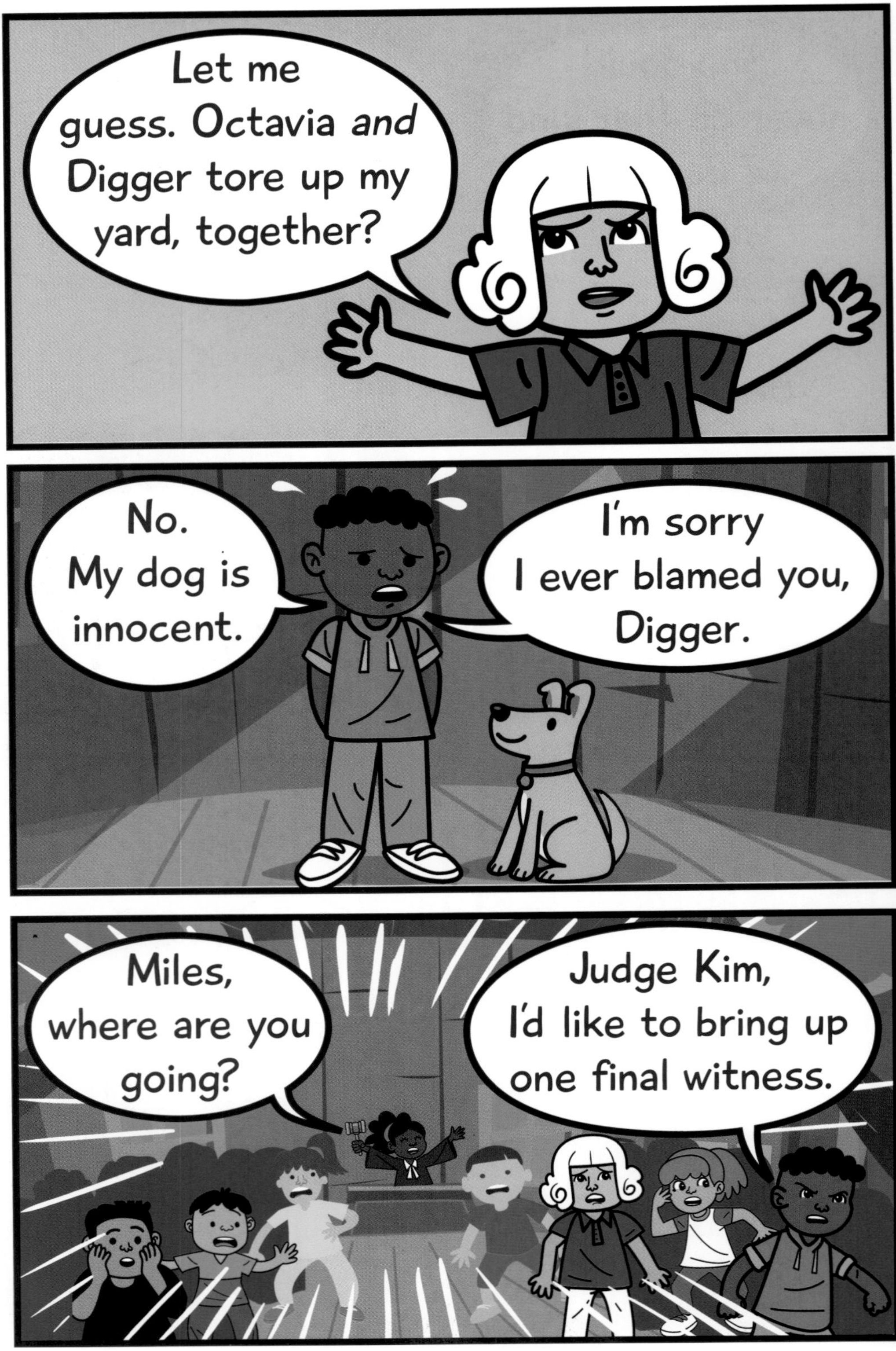
Let me guess. Octavia *and* Digger tore up my yard, together?
No. My dog is innocent.
I'm sorry I ever blamed you, Digger.
Miles, where are you going?
Judge Kim, I'd like to bring up one final witness.

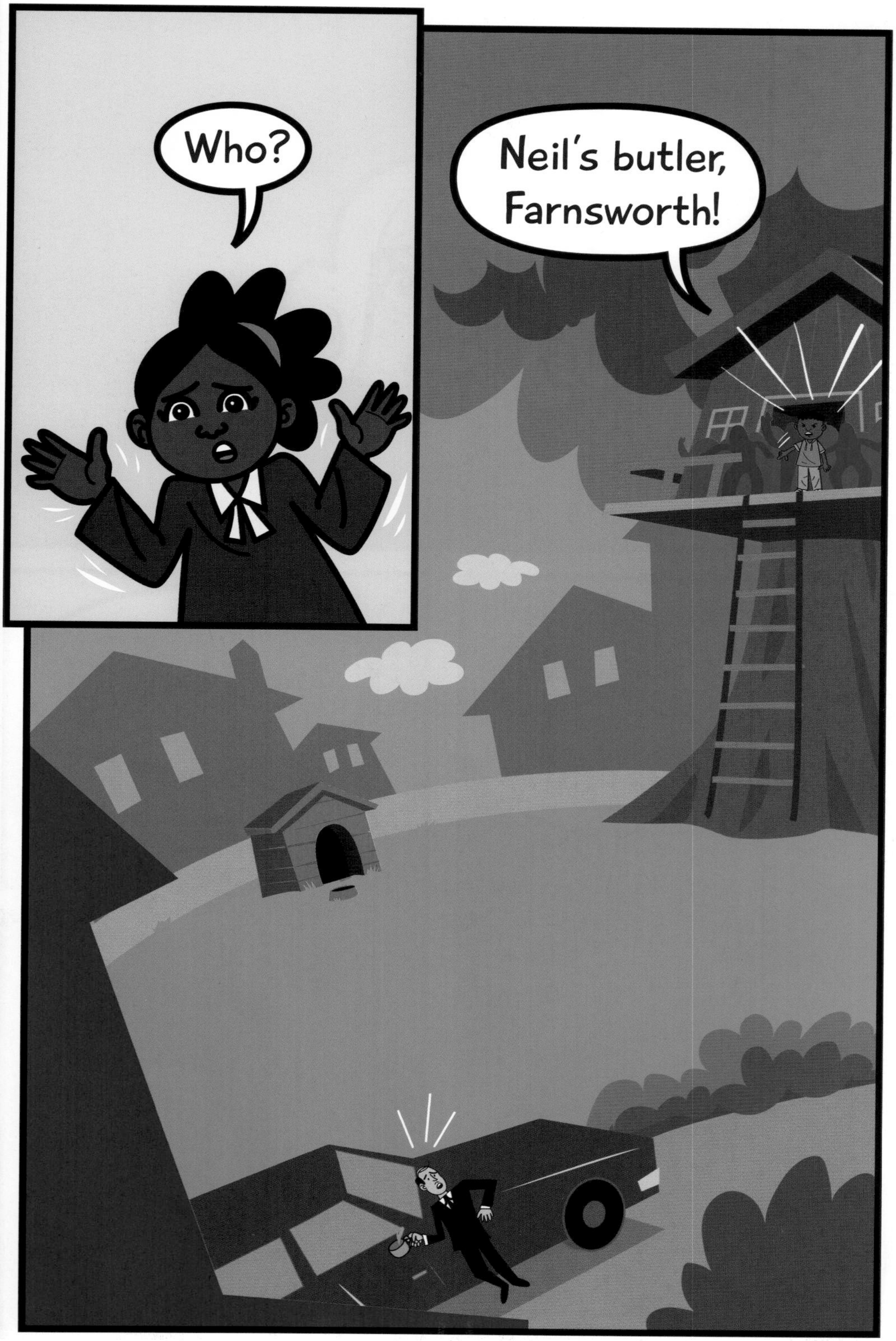
Who?
Neil's butler, Farnsworth!

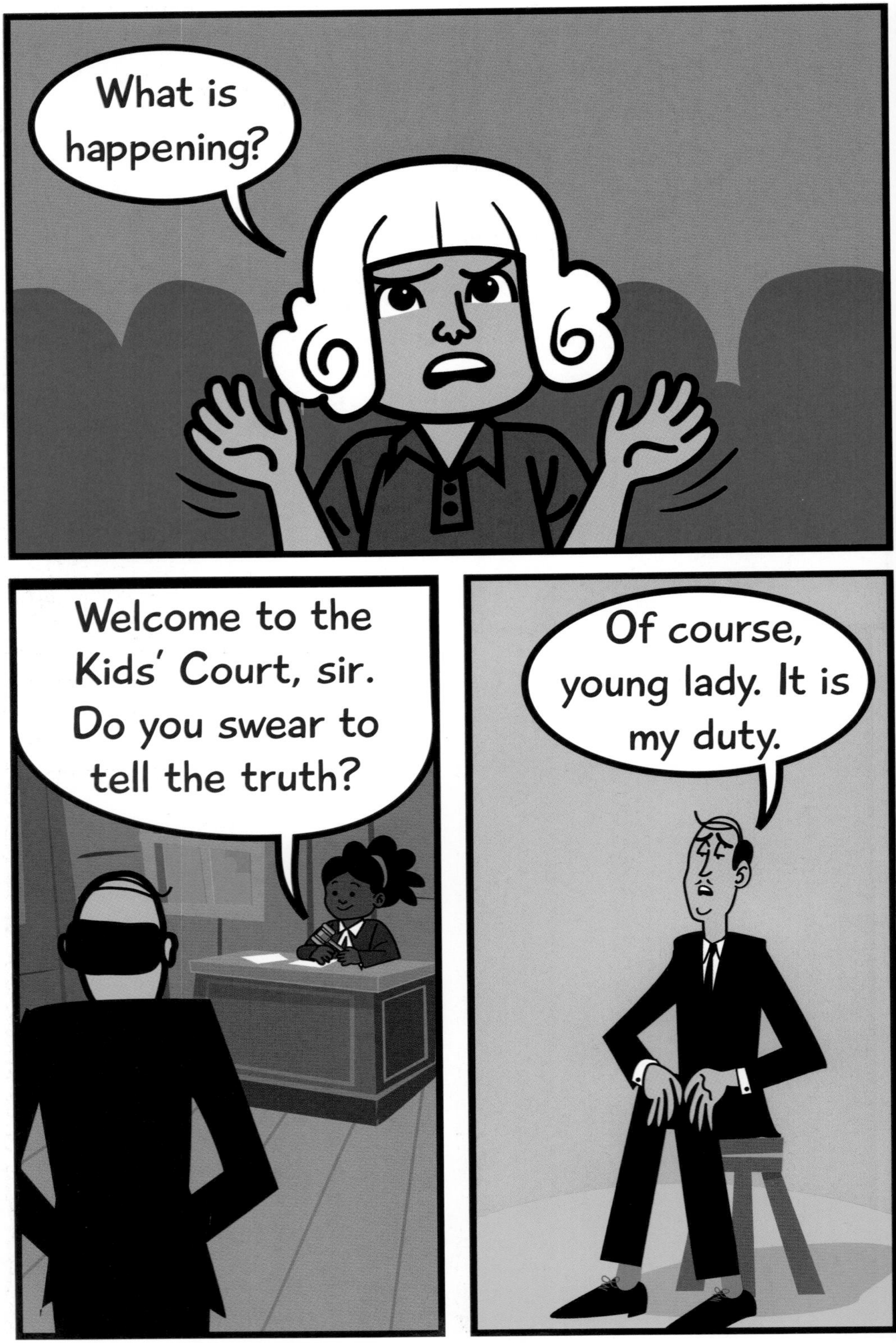
What is happening?
Welcome to the Kids' Court, sir. Do you swear to tell the truth?
Of course, young lady. It is my duty.

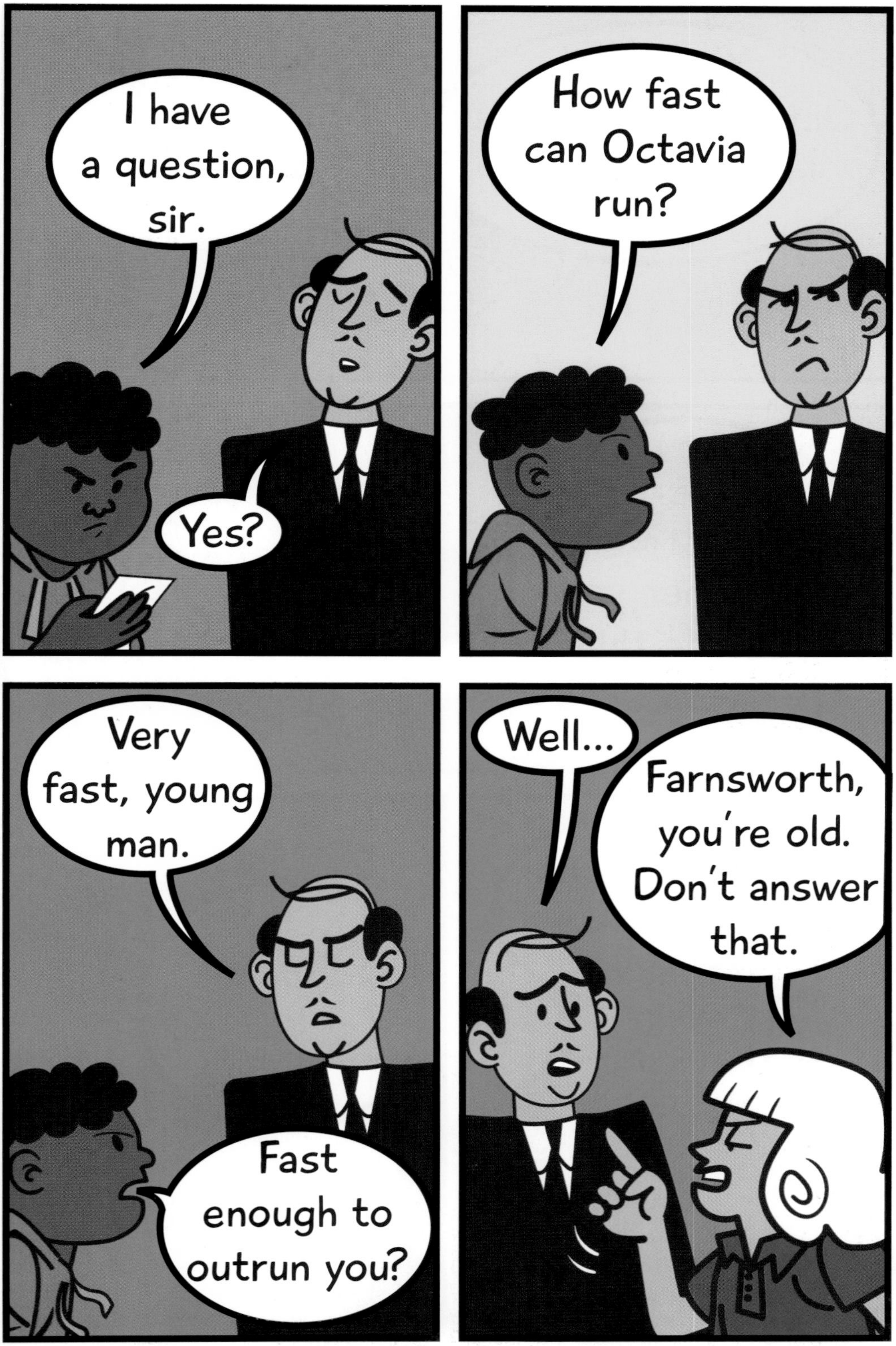
I have a question, sir.
Yes?
How fast can Octavia run?
Very fast, young man.
Fast enough to outrun you?
Well...
Farnsworth, you're old. Don't answer that.

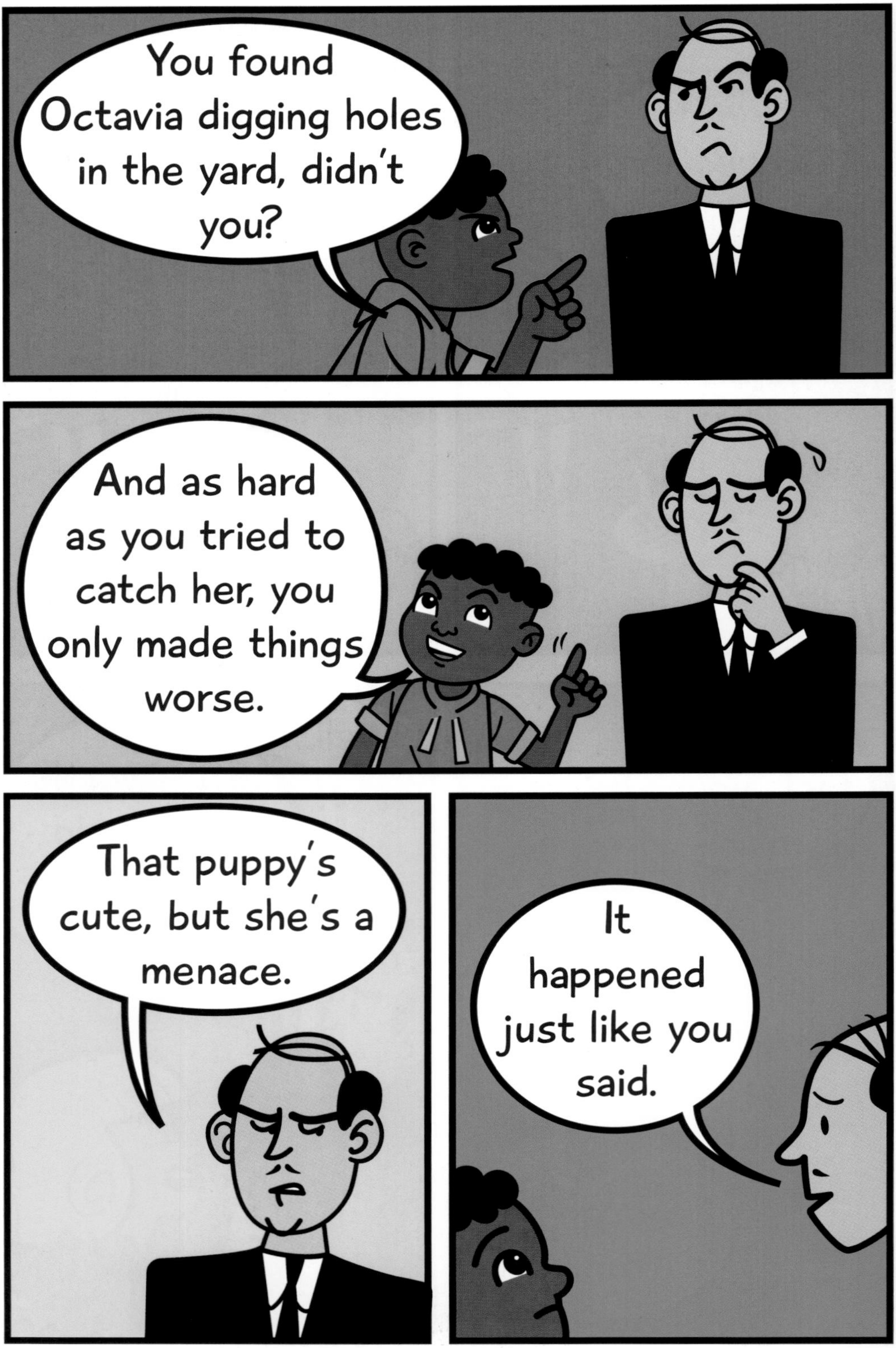
You found Octavia digging holes in the yard, didn't you?
And as hard as you tried to catch her, you only made things worse.
That puppy's cute, but she's a menace.
It happened just like you said.

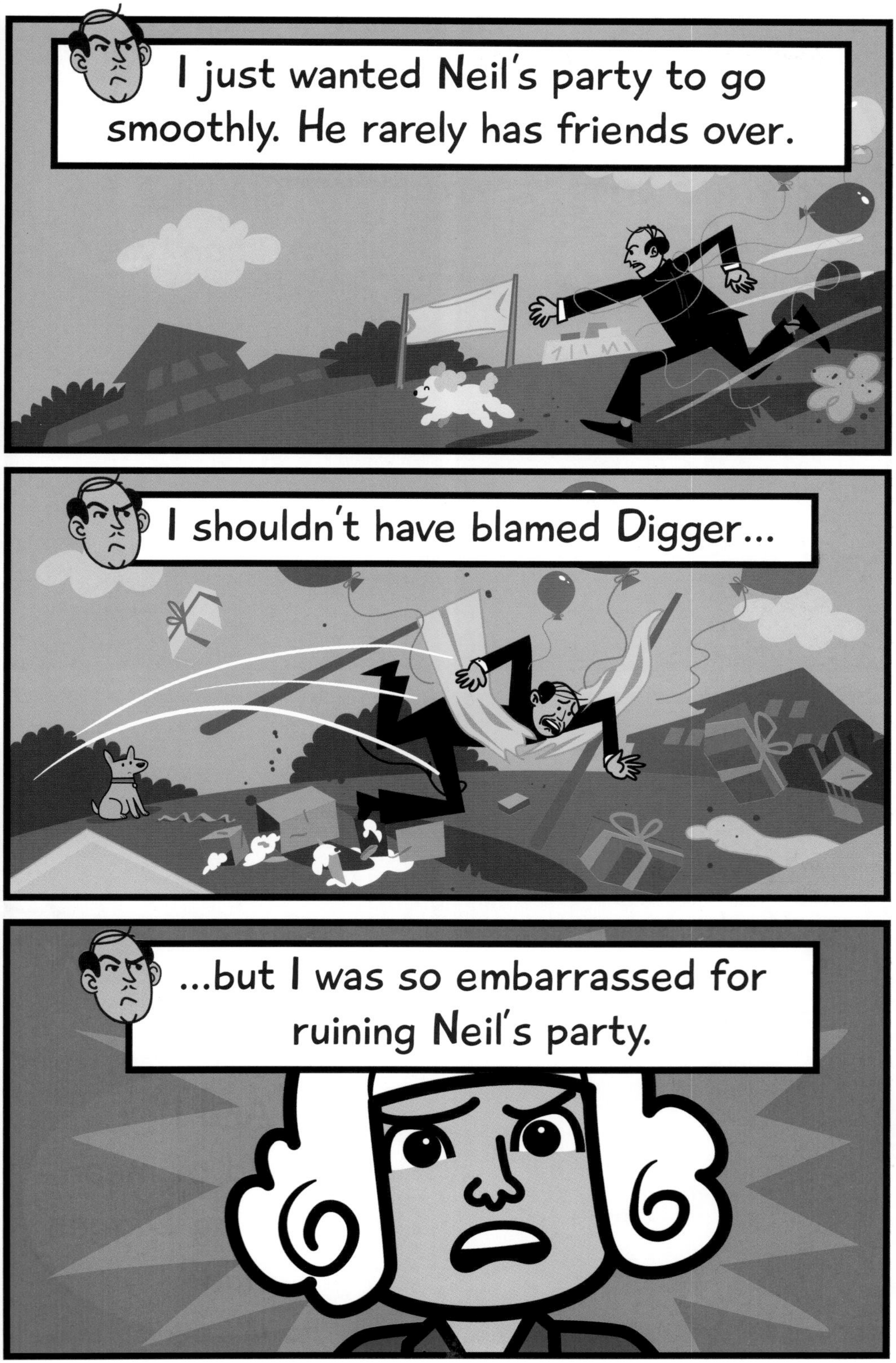
I just wanted Neil's party to go smoothly. He rarely has friends over.
I shouldn't have blamed Digger...
...but I was so embarrassed for ruining Neil's party.

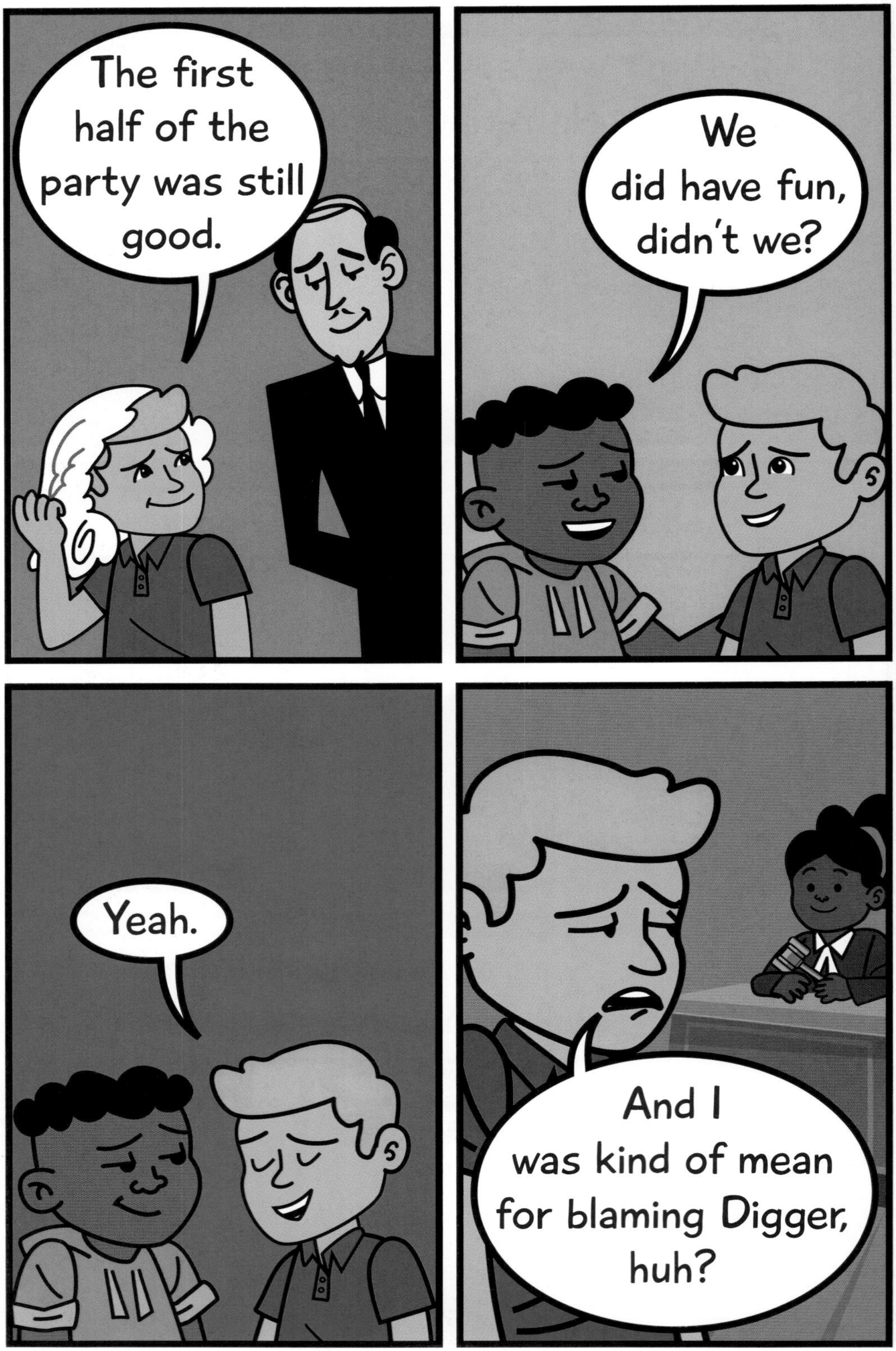
The first half of the party was still good.
We did have fun, didn't we?
Yeah.
And I was kind of mean for blaming Digger, huh?

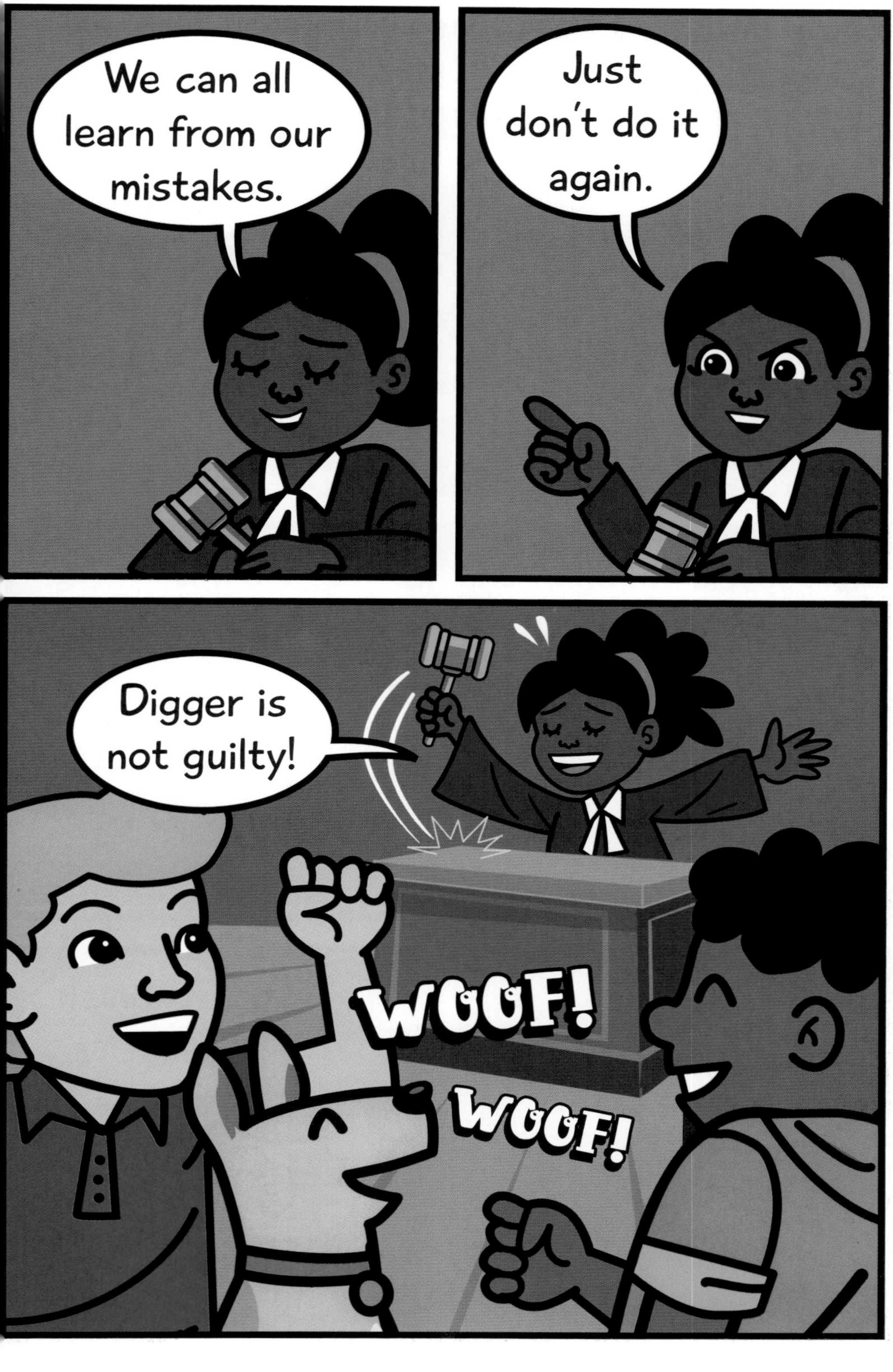
We can all learn from our mistakes.
Just don't do it again.
Digger is not guilty!
WOOF!
WOOF!

After court Neil decides to take his friends for a ride.

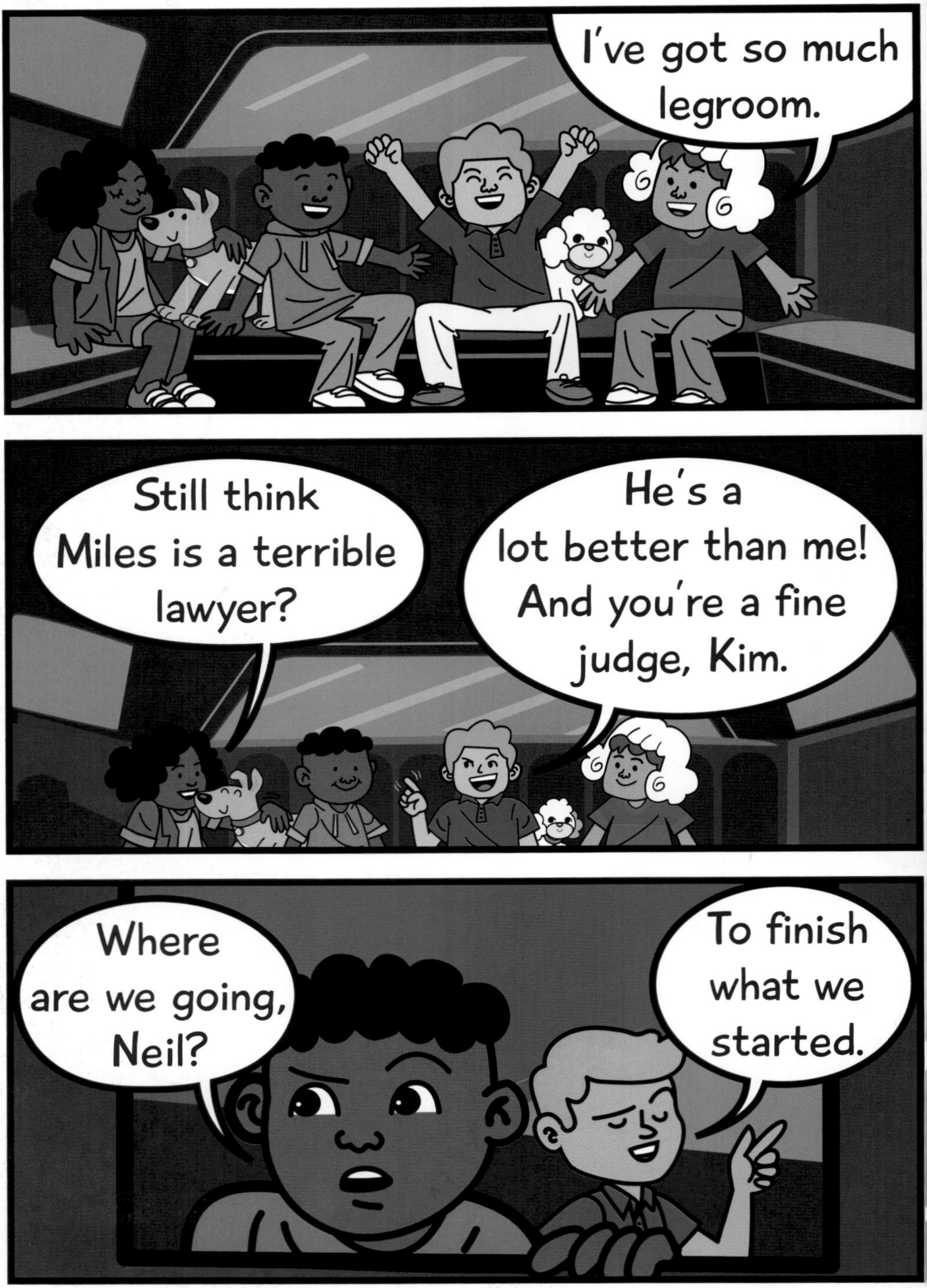
I've got so much legroom.
Still think Miles is a terrible lawyer?
He's a lot better than me! And you're a fine judge, Kim.
Where are we going, Neil?
To finish what we started.

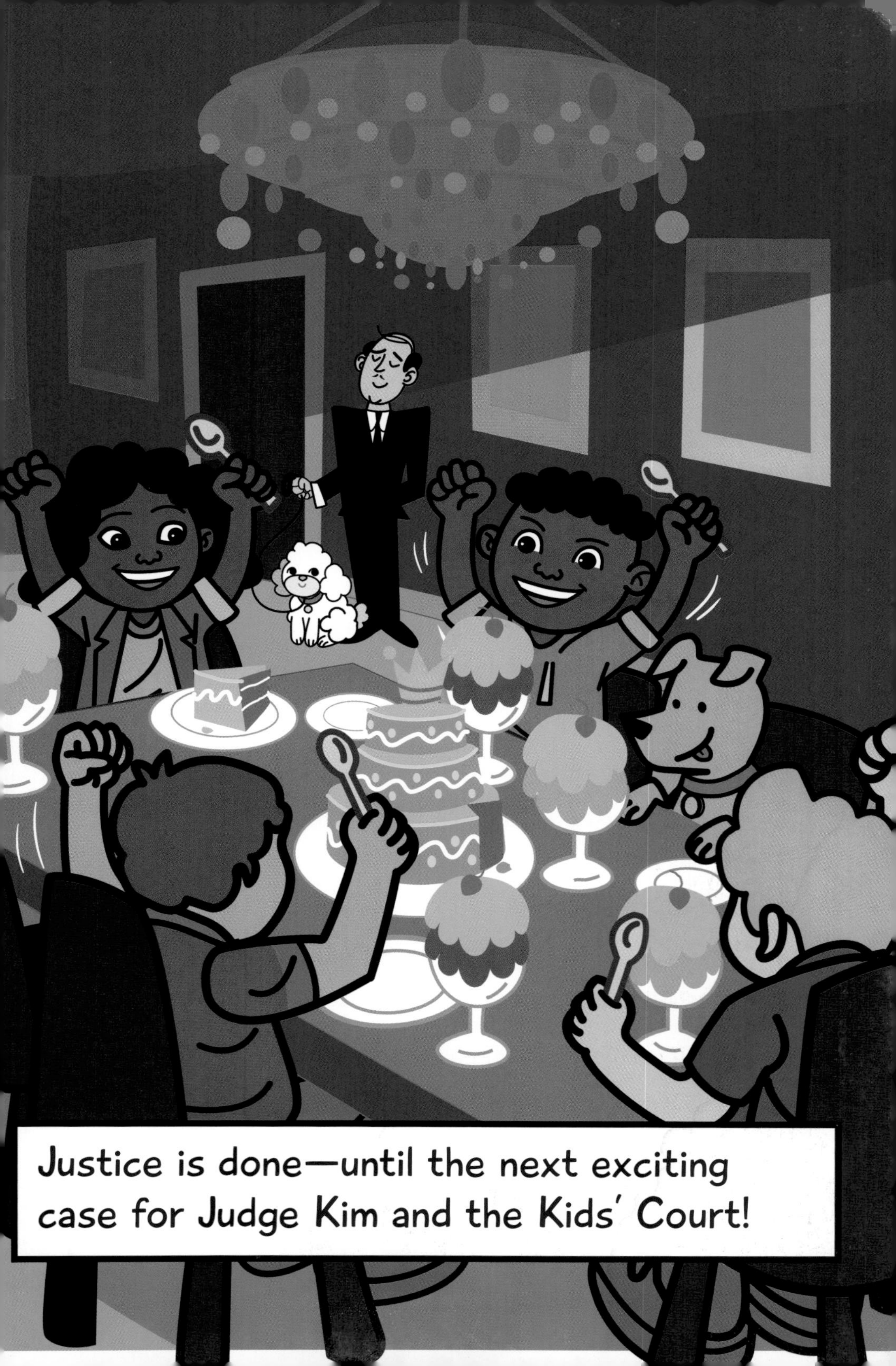
Justice is done—until the next exciting case for Judge Kim and the Kids' Court!

GLOSSARY

<u>case</u>: a disagreement between two people or groups that is decided in court.

<u>court</u>: a place where a judge listens to and decides on cases.

<u>defendant</u>: a person who is brought to court because they are accused of doing something wrong.

<u>evidence</u>: information presented in court to help a judge understand a case.

<u>judge</u>: a person who listens to cases and decides who is right and who is wrong.

<u>justice</u>: when a proper punishment or fair treatment is given by a judge.

<u>lawyer</u>: a person who helps people present their side in court. Then the judge can decide who wins the case.

<u>trial</u>: when a case is brought to court to decide whether or not a person has broken the law.

<u>witness</u>: a person who saw something happen that is related to a case.

Note to readers: Some of these words may have more than one definition. The definitions above match how these words are used in this book.

THE INDIAN IN THE CUPBOARD

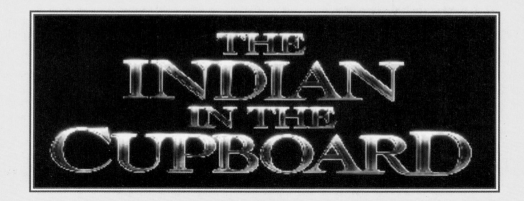

Omri's Scrapbook

Adapted by Nancy E. Krulik
From the movie *The Indian in the Cupboard*
Screenplay by Melissa Mathison based on the novel by Lynne Reid Banks

SCHOLASTIC INC.
New York Toronto London Auckland Sydney

For Ian Zachary

ISBN 0-590-50983-7

Copyright © 1995 by Paramount Pictures
All rights reserved. Published by Scholastic Inc.
Adapted from the movie *The Indian in the Cupboard*
Screenplay by Melissa Mathison, based upon the novel by Lynne Reid Banks.

12 11 10 9 8 7 6 5 4 3 2 1   5 6 7 8 9/9 0/0

Printed in the U.S.A   24

First Scholastic printing, July 1995

It all started on my birthday. . . .

At first, this birthday seemed like all my other birthdays.
My mom baked a cake and my dad made my brothers sing
"Happy Birthday" to me.

Gillon

Mom

Adiel

Dad

5

I got some really neat stuff. My parents even gave me a top-of-the-line
skateboard...with a helmet, of course!
My best friend, Patrick, gave me a plastic Indian figure. It was kind of
a cool gift.

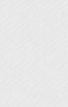

6

Patrick said the Indian reminded him of me.
I'm not sure how.

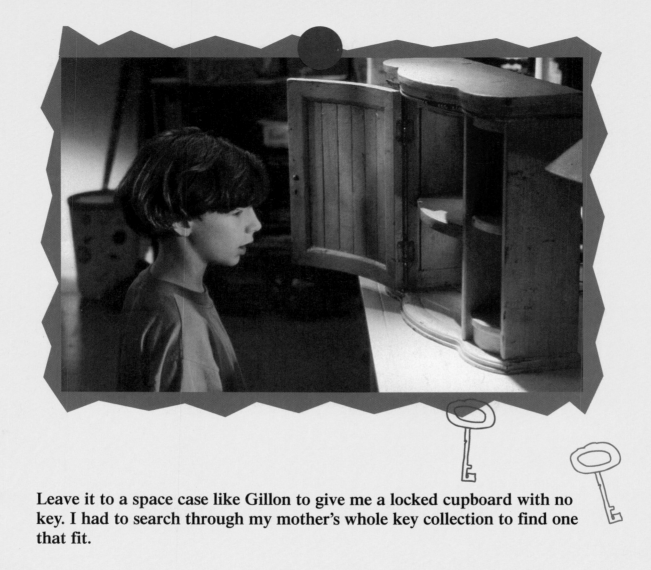

Leave it to a space case like Gillon to give me a locked cupboard with no key. I had to search through my mother's whole key collection to find one that fit.

The key belonged to my mom's grandmother (which I think means it belonged to my great-grandmother). The key was very important to my mom. I had to promise I wouldn't lose it.

I tried putting a bunch of toys in the cupboard. The new Indian was the first one I found that could fit. I put him in and locked the door.

He's alive!

Later, when I opened the door, I nearly fell over dead!

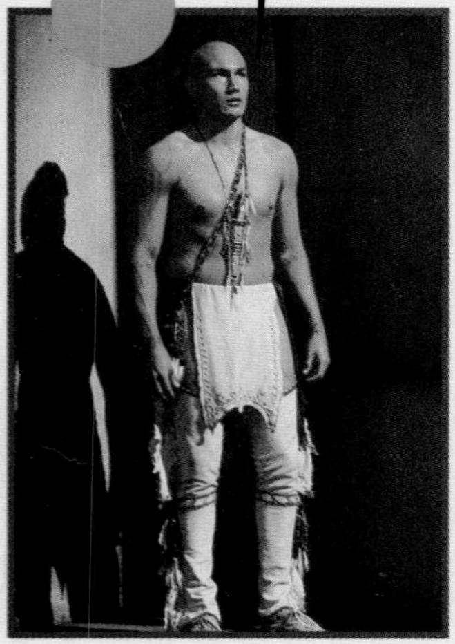
Giant!

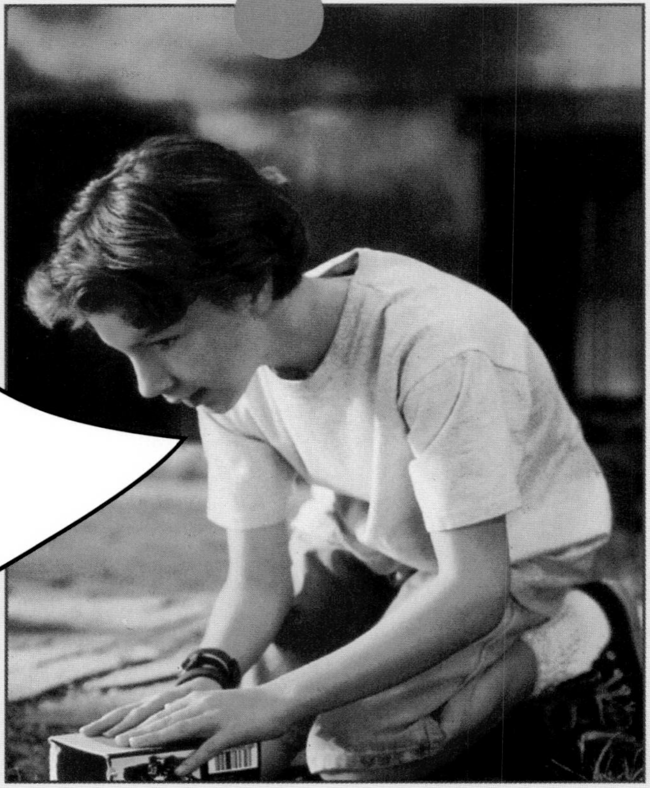
I am not a giant. You're just small.

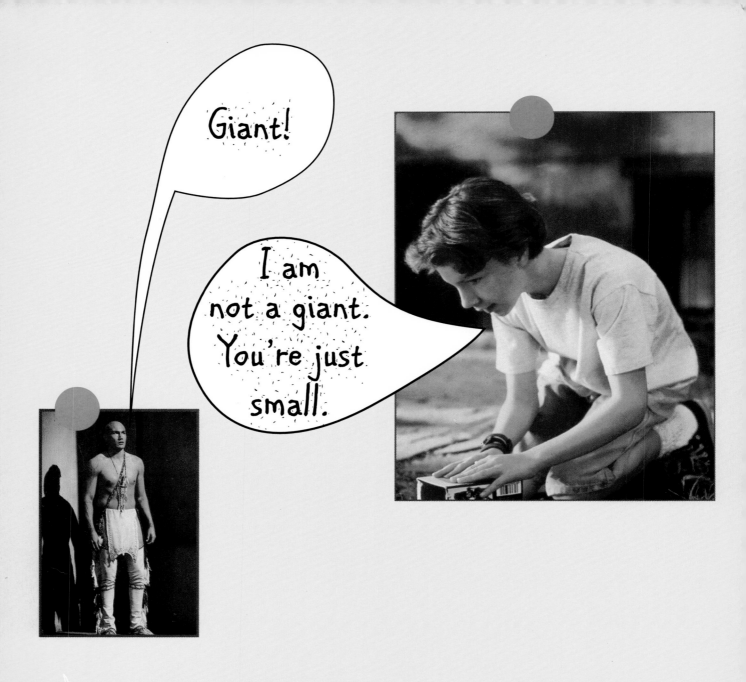

Together, the key and the cupboard could bring toys to life. At first that was fun. Then I realized I needed to be careful.

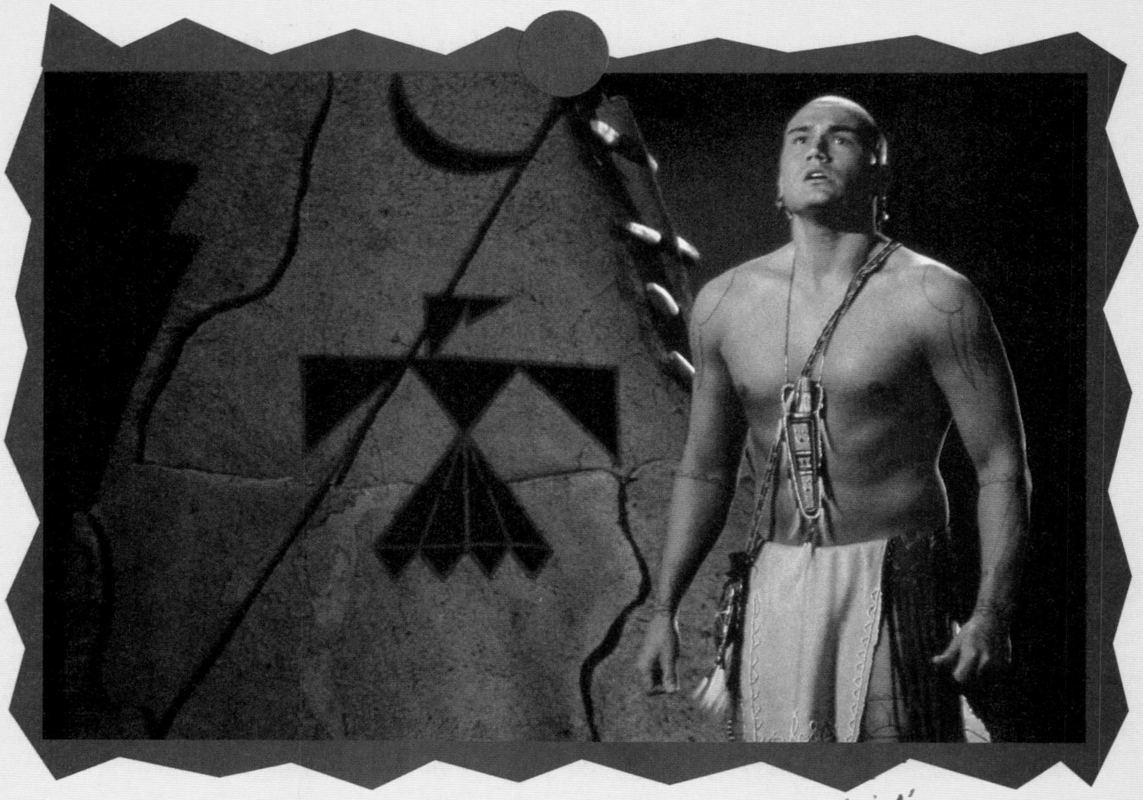

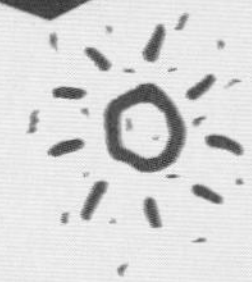

The Indian was an Onondaga gah. That means he belonged to the Iroquois Confederacy. His name was Oh gwai, which means Little Bear. Little Bear needed a place to live. I gave him a toy tepee.

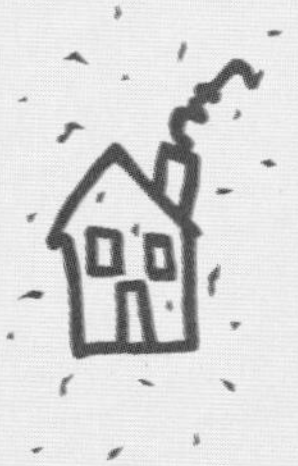

What I didn't know was that the Iroquois live in longhouses.

What I've Learned About the Iroquois
1. These are the six nations that make up the Iroquois Confederacy: Mohawk, Oneida, Onondaga, Cayuga, Seneca, Tuscarora.
2. The tribes joined together to stop a war.
3. The Iroquois have their own government, called a tribal council, with its own laws.
4. Women are in charge of the tribal council.
5. The Iroquois have a lot of respect for nature and magic.

The great tree has lived into the future!

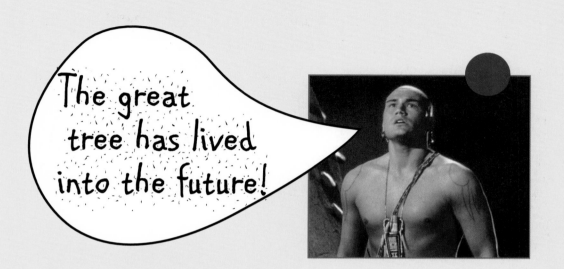

Little Bear was used to living in 1761. A lot of things have changed since then. I think Little Bear was glad to discover some things had not.

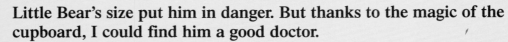

Little Bear's size put him in danger. But thanks to the magic of the cupboard, I could find him a good doctor.

I also had to protect him from my brothers...

and large animals.

I had to keep the magic of the cupboard a secret. It would be dangerous if the wrong people found out about it.
The only person I trusted enough to tell was my best pal, Patrick.
Soon, Patrick wanted a little friend of his own.

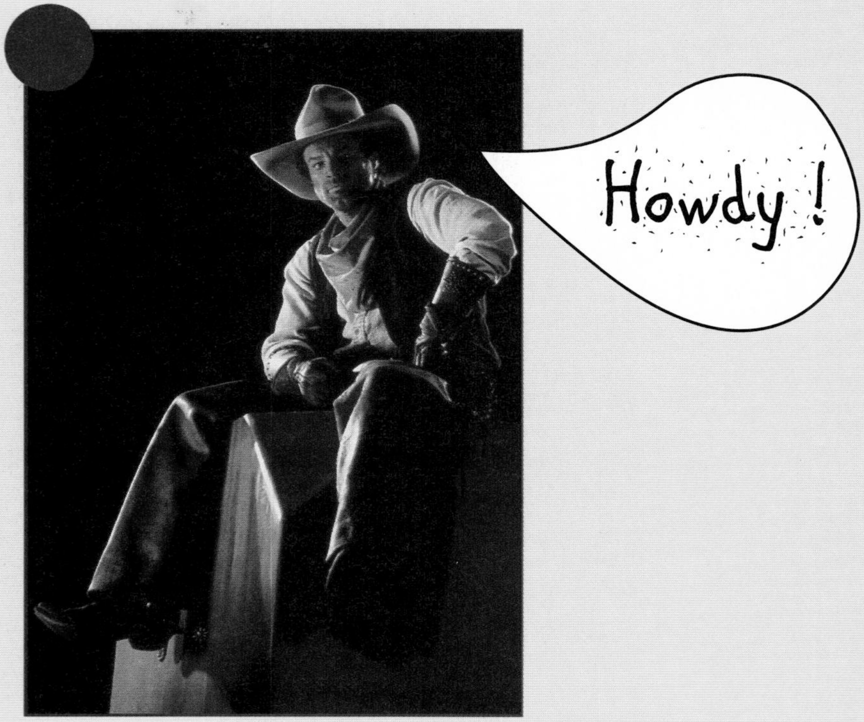
Howdy !

Boone, who lived in 1789, was pretty shocked to find himself alive in 1995!

At first Boone and Little Bear didn't get along.

But once they got to know each other they became best buddies—sort of like me and Patrick.

When I was in school, I worried
about Little Bear all the time.
So, I started bringing him with me.

One day, Little Bear performed
an ancient Iroquois ceremony.

26

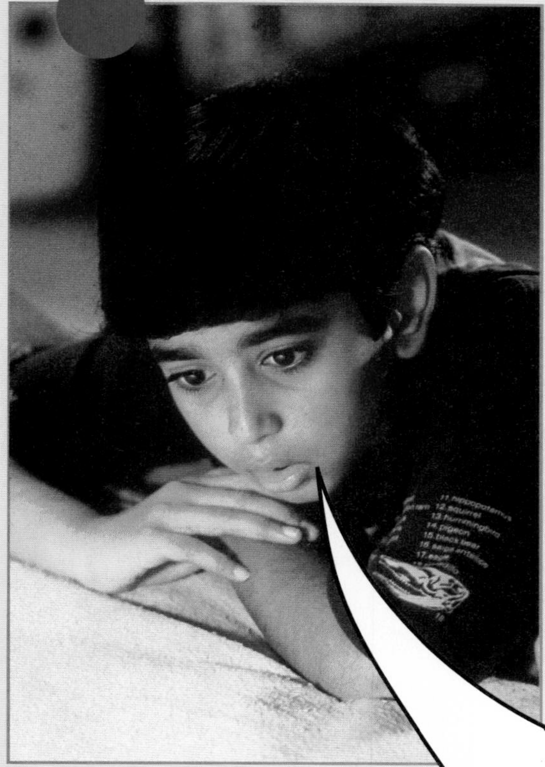

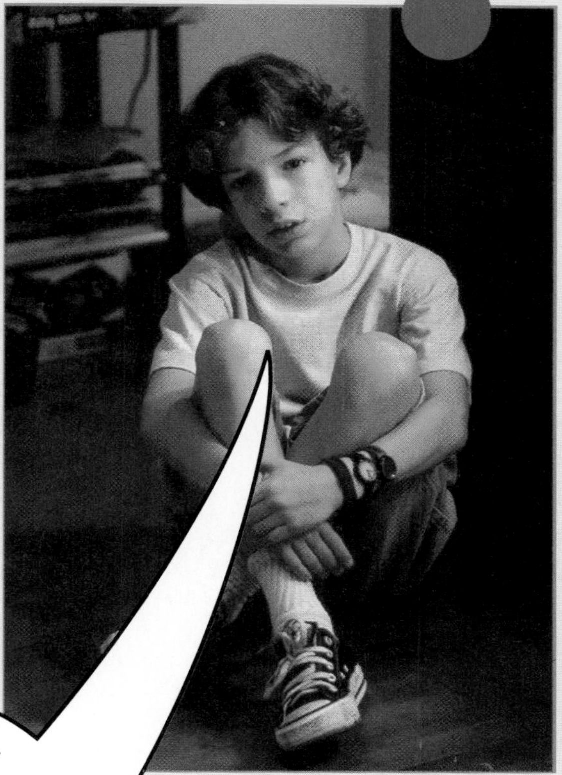

We are ready to learn, Little Bear.

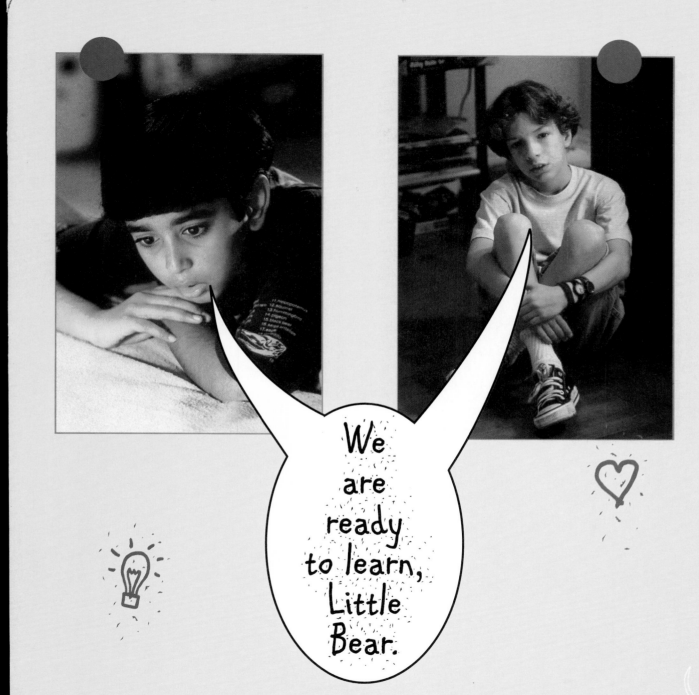

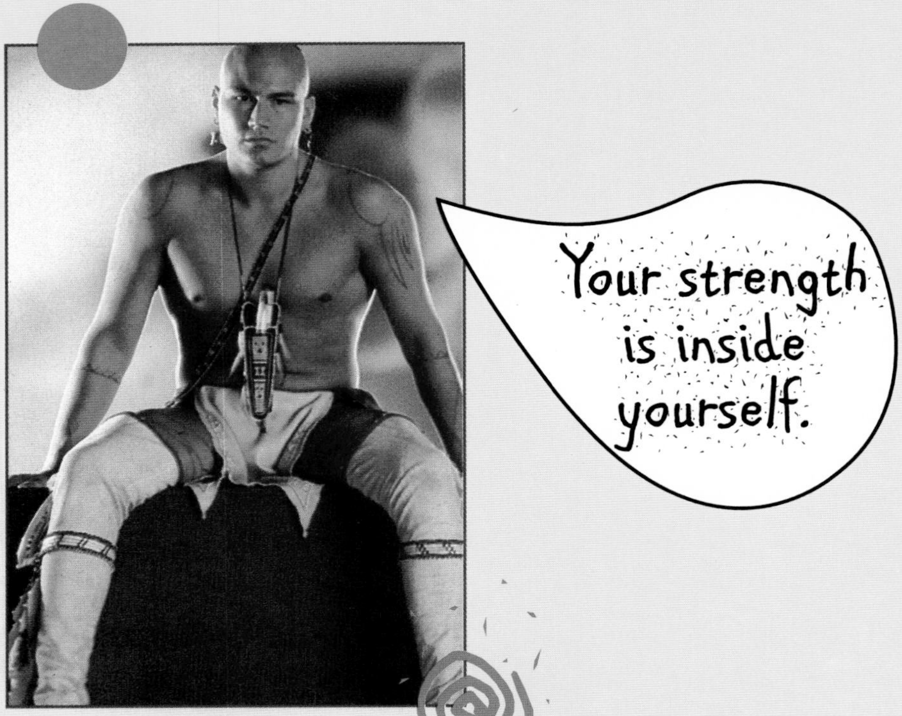
Your strength is inside yourself.

Little Bear explained the great teachings of the Onondaga gah.

Deep down I knew that
Little Bear would have to go
home pretty soon.

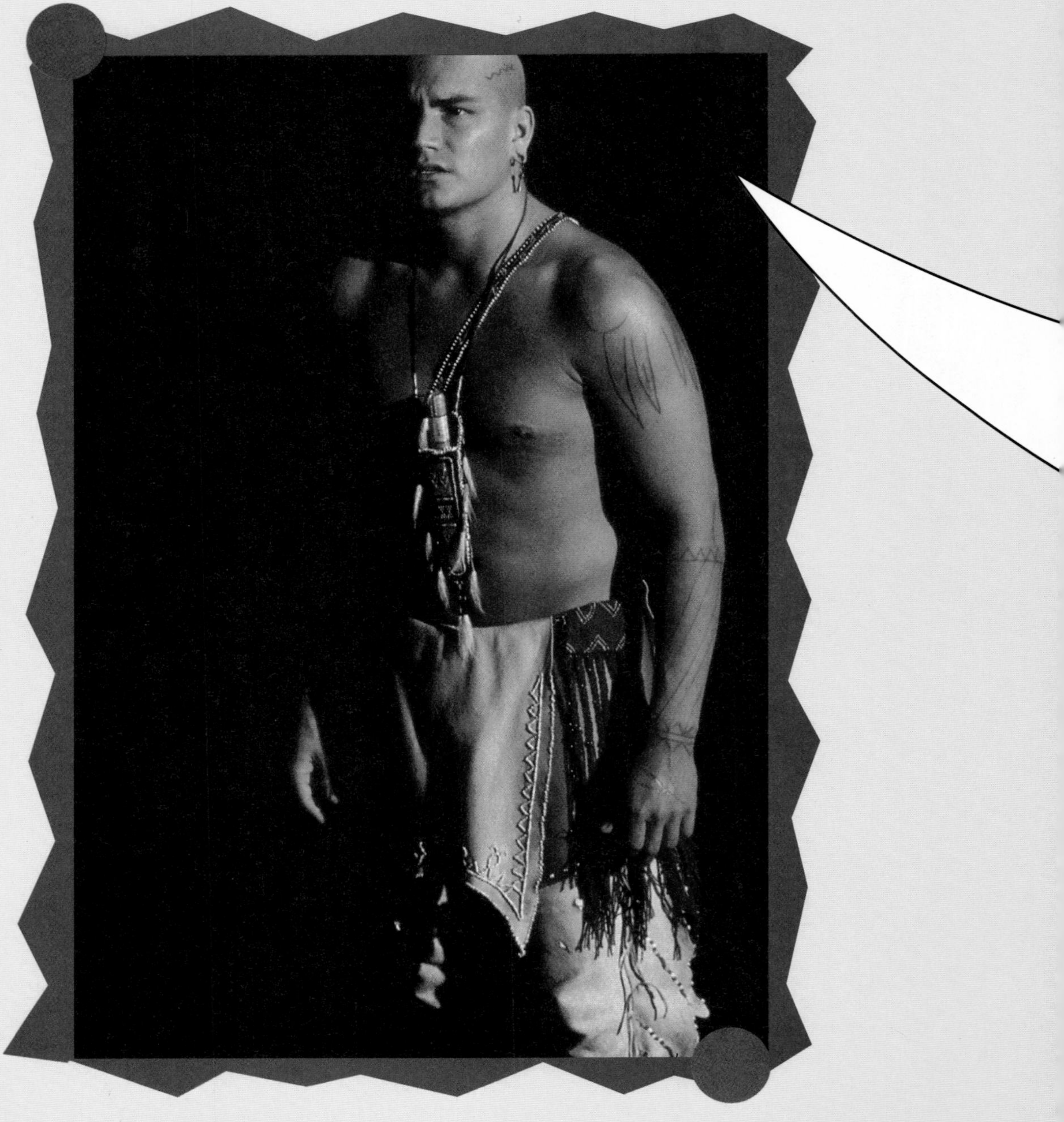

I must go back to my people and my time. And Boone must go to his.

I don't worry about Little Bear anymore. He's with his own people, in his own time. I know that someday he will be a great leader.